*Worried About
Diablo*

Gabi Adam

Worried About
Diablo

Copyright © 2004 Gaby Adam
The plot and the names of the characters are entirely fictional
Original title: *Sorge um Diabolo*
Published by PonyClub, Stabenfeldt A/S
Coverphoto: Bob Langrish
Coverlayout: Stabenfeldt A/S
Translated by Barclay House Publishing
Edited by Karen Pasacreta
Printing: GGP Media, Germany 2004

ISBN 82-591-1151-9

For Gypsy, Chubby, and Sweetie,
three wonderful horses in my life

Chapter 1

Ricki Sulai lay on her stomach in the meadow behind the old farmhouse her parents had recently bought. Beside her lay her friends Cathy, Kevin, and Lillian. A little farther off, their horses and Chico, the Bates family donkey, were grazing in their huge paddock on the meadow. They moved very slowly on this warm summer day.

"The past few days have been really great, don't you think?" said Cathy Sutherland. She yawned with pleasure and, as she closed her eyes, let her head slowly sink down onto her crossed arms.

"Yeah," agreed Kevin, who was leafing through a magazine for young equestrians.

Ricki glanced over his shoulder, curious, while she cuddled against him.

"So far, we've really been lucky with the weather during this summer vacation," she said.

Lillian nodded. "But sometimes it's been almost too hot. There hasn't been a storm in a long time."

"If you're anxious for a storm, all you have to do is ask Ricki's tidy mother to describe the condition of her room.

Until yesterday, at least, it looked like a tornado had passed through it," grinned Kevin.

Ricki groaned and rolled over onto her back. "Don't remind me about my room! Mom threatened to have a garbage truck come while I was gone and throw everything away that supposedly doesn't belong in a girl's room... Just imagine how boring it would be then. After all, I'm really attached to my stuff."

"I can understand that," Lillian Bates laughed. "I'd feel the same way, but I'd try to convince parents how important it is to save old horseshoes and old riding boots full of holes, or to put up all kinds of horse pictures, photos, and posters on the walls. Sometimes it seems like our parents have forgotten they were ever young themselves." Lillian rolled over onto her back, too, and put her arms behind her head.

She enjoyed this peaceful moment with her eyes closed. Then, from a short distance away, the 15-year-old heard Diablo's whinny. He must be bothered by the loud noise her father's tractor was making as he drove over the meadow, shattering the blessed silence.

Diablo hated these huge vehicles.

Ricki laughed. Without even looking, she knew that her horse would now run along the paddock fence with his ears laid back until Dave Bates had gone a good distance away from them.

Doc Holliday, Lillian's white horse, on the other hand, was completely uninterested. He dozed in the shade of the huge pear tree, just like Chico. Rashid and Sharazan, however, stood next to each other like tall statues and observed Diablo.

Ricki was endlessly grateful that her parents had moved

6

the family to the country. It meant that finally she had her own stable for Diablo, with enough space for her friends' horses as well as the Bates's little donkey.

Kevin, who owned Sharazan, and Cathy, the caretaker for Rashid who belonged to the former circus rider Carlotta Mancini, came to the Sulai farm every day on their bikes to get together with Ricki and Lillian, who lived close by. The friends were like a four-leaf clover, since they were almost always together in the afternoon.

Today, they would probably saddle their horses again and go for an extended ride through the nearby fields, something they found totally enjoyable.

"Ricki Sulai! Would it be possible for you to take your elbow out of my back? It's really starting to hurt!" Kevin twisted himself around like an eel, but his girlfriend just laughed and gave him a little kiss on the cheek before she slid sideways.

"Of course, Mr. Thomas! What have you been reading all this time? You haven't turned the page in ages!"

Ricki pulled the magazine out of his hands with a tug.

"Oh, that thing is older than the hills!" she said, and allowed Kevin to take the magazine back.

"You can win a riding vacation! That would be great, wouldn't it?"

Lillian made a face. "Don't tell me you actually sent something in?" she asked. "Why do *you* need a riding vacation? You have your own horse in your girlfriend's stable and can go riding every day. Isn't that enough for you?"

"I guess so," Kevin answered reflectively. "But I wouldn't have anything against a real riding vacation, with all the extras, and on an island in the Caribbean."

"You would really go riding on a beautiful beach while

your Sharazan grows roots here? Hard to believe," Cathy joined in, suddenly wide awake.

"I think he would survive the seven days. After all, he isn't alone in the paddock, and with Jake's good care I wouldn't need to worry about him at all!"

Jake, who had given Diablo to Ricki as a gift, lived in the cottage across from the house on the property Ricki's parents Marcus and Brigitte had bought, and he had volunteered to do the work in the stable. The old stable master, who had become like family, had worked around horses all his life and he enjoyed taking care of the four horses and the little donkey every day. He knew so much about horses and loved to share what he knew. The kids had learned a lot from him.

"Wow! A riding vacation on an island! That would be great, but I don't know if I could stand to be away from Diablo for a whole week!" Ricki glanced happily over to the paddock. As though her horse had sensed that she was talking about him, he stretched his head up high and stared back at her. His loud whinny alerted his fellow horses.

"Just look at those beautiful creatures! Do you know how lucky we all are?" For Ricki, every day with Diablo was like a miracle, and there was nothing in the world she would trade for her beloved black horse.

The rustling of the magazine as Kevin folded it closed, pulled her out of her daydream.

"I don't think I have to worry about leaving Sharazan alone," Kevin chuckled. He fanned some air onto his face with the magazine and then got up. "After all, I've never won anything before!"

But Cathy wouldn't let him off the hook. "That definitely means you entered the contest, or am I wrong?"

Kevin nodded.

"And what if you *do* win? Who would you take along?" Lillian wanted to know. "Those kinds of prizes are usually for two people."

"Don't say the wrong thing!" grinned Ricki, and wagged her finger at her boyfriend.

"Well, since you don't want to leave Diablo here alone, I'll have to think about it," he said and stretched. "We'll talk about it again if it happens, okay?"

"Okay!" answered Ricki easily and got up as well. "Let's go into the house and get something cold to drink. I'm dying of thirst. You all must be too?"

"You bet!"

"Let's go!"

"So, let's raid Mom's refrigerator. Hopefully there's some iced tea or lemonade lurking there." Ricki ran ahead to look for the cool beverage, while her friends followed more slowly.

A little while later, the four friends were sitting around the heavy wooden table in the big kitchen, drinking huge glasses of delicious, refreshing peach iced tea. They had already forgotten the riding vacation and were now planning their ride together.

"Vacations are wonderful!" said Cathy, handing Ricki her empty glass. "Can I have some more tea? This stuff is *sooo* good!"

"Of course! Just keep pouring in the calories!" Ricki teased. "But be careful that you don't have to jump out of the saddle 10 times when the tea has run through you!"

Lillian and Kevin laughed at the thought.

"Nevertheless, give me that drink! At the worst, we may have to make a few pit stops. Where are we going to ride today? There's always stuff going on around Echo Lake."

"Josh asked if we wanted to visit him," Lillian said nonchalantly, finishing off the last of her iced tea. "He would join us with Cherish, and we could all ride to the old quarry. He said he found an ammonite fossil there the other day."

As she looked around at her friends, who were two years younger than she, and saw the smiles on their faces, Lillian knew exactly what they were thinking.

It's always Josh this and Josh that...that's the way it is when you're in love!

Lillian had become the girlfriend of 17-year-old Joshua Cole one week ago. He rode Western style and attracted a lot of attention when he rode around on his little spotted mare. Just the tooled Western saddle alone was gorgeous, and with his Stetson hat and his fringed leather chaps, he looked every inch a cowboy on the rodeo circuit.

He often tapped his finger on his Stetson, made Cherish rear up with a certain pressure from his thigh, then rode on as though nothing had happened. Meanwhile, everyone who saw him thought immediately of the hero in every Western movie they had ever seen.

Lillian was very proud of Josh, who could ride Cherish with such ease and loose reins.

"I'll never ride any other way," the Western-style rider had said, and Lillian was already considering whether she should train her Holli in this style, too. But she doubted the huge Hanoverian would be suitable as a Western-style horse.

"There's one good thing about your being Josh's girlfriend," Ricki said with a wink. "In the future, you'll probably get a discount on all the riding equipment you need. What luck, really, that Josh's father owns the riding shop in town. By the way, I could use a new brush and comb."

"My boots aren't in great shape either," Kevin added, but Lillian just smiled at them with false pity.

"How pathetic. I can't believe I'm surrounded by parasites. But we'll see. I'll talk with Josh…maybe you'll get a discount for buying so much!"

"That would be great!" Kevin yawned, then he suddenly remembered what Lillian had said a minute ago.

"Did you say Josh found an ammonite? Around here? That's almost impossible!" Kevin shook his head in disbelief.

"He did! I haven't seen it yet, but—"

"We'll definitely have to look at it. If there are more of these snail fossils in the quarry, it would be a sensation. The town would definitely be interested," Cathy gushed. But Kevin said no.

"I don't care about the town! I would love to have a stone like that. It fascinates me to think that these petrified objects are millions of years old."

"I didn't know you were interested in old stones?" Ricki cleared away the glasses and then sat back down at the table. "But if you want to, we'll go look for these ammonites today. Maybe we'll be lucky!" she said.

"Okay, that's settled! I'll call Josh at home and tell him that we're coming." Lillian's eyes beamed. "Maybe he can bring the fossil to the stable so we can see it."

"I'm sure you won't look at the fossil even once!" joked Ricki. "You won't be able to take your eyes off Josh!"

"It's no wonder, Lillian replied. "Ancient petrified snails don't have the charm of a 17-year-old Western-style rider!"

"Well, if we let you explain Josh's charm, we won't have time to go riding today," Cathy said. She earned a punch from her girlfriend, who got up nonetheless.

"She's right," admitted Lillian and turned to Ricki. "Can I phone him from here?" she asked.

Ricki shrugged her shoulders. "I have no idea if you can. You have to take down the receiver—that's the thing you speak into—but be careful, if the cord is on top, then you're holding it upside down, and—"

Lillian groaned and rolled her eyes upward. "Man, you are so weird!" she said before disappearing into the next room to make the date with Josh.

"I think we can get going in about two hours," said Kevin. "The two of them will need about that much time to go over the particulars. After all, they just saw each other yesterday."

Cathy giggled, but before she could respond, Lillian was back.

"All set, we can. Is something the matter?" she asked, baffled by her friends' surprised expressions.

"No, no," laughed Kevin, getting out of his chair, "everything's just fine. Luckily I didn't make any bets on how long your phone call would last."

In good spirits, the teenagers left the kitchen and started toward the stable. Armed with lead ropes, they ran down to the paddock to get the animals.

"It's about time for us to get going," said Cathy. She stroked Rashid's forehead lovingly before she tied up the dun to lead him to the stable. "Great, he's not even dirty to-day," she said happily. Lillian observed her Holli with a sigh.

"I think I'm going to have to dye him another color one day. He's more brown than white. Holli, you're a little pig," she chastised.

"Pigs are pink!" Kevin reminded her as he began to brush his horse.

"Okay, that's enough name calling and squabbling. Chico's still a child! We don't want him to learn bad manners," Ricki joked as she came out of the tack room with her grooming basket. As she groomed her Diablo, she thought again about the riding vacation contest. Would Kevin really go if he won?

As the friends rode around the banks of Echo Lake, a warm breeze came up, just enough to relieve the stifling summer heat.

"Oh, that feels good!" Ricki closed her eyes in pleasure. "When we were riding through the fields before, it felt as though the air was standing still!"

"But the mosquitoes are much worse here at the lake!" Kevin grumbled and slapped his arm for the umpteenth time with the palm of his other hand. "Darn, missed again!"

"You're a real animal activist," Lillian teased him, and Kevin got back by making a horrible, funny-looking face.

"Protecting animals is the last thing I would do where these beasts are concerned. If I had my way, these insects wouldn't even exist!"

"Oh, stop being such a grouch," Ricki interrupted her boyfriend. "Just enjoy this wonderful day and the beautiful scenery around us," she indicated the scenery with a sweep of her hand. "I love this lake! I could stare at the water for hours."

"*You* try to enjoy something, when you're covered with bites," growled Kevin, but Ricki had decided to pay no attention to him.

"You know what? Maybe there's a solution. Let's see if our horses are fast enough to outrun the mosquitoes."

"Great idea! Let's ride!"

"Holli, let's go!"

With these words the mosquitoes and everything else on the teens' minds disappeared as they urged their horses into a light gallop along the edge of the lake.

The animals sprang ahead with the enormous strength of their bodies, yet they seemed to float weightlessly over the path, which was wide and open in front of them. It was as though horses and riders just let themselves go and enjoy the feel of the wind in their faces, far away from any worries.

Ricki sat lightly on Diablo and leaned way over his neck. She experienced a wondrous joy of freedom rise within her. She was also filled with enormous thankfulness that this wonderful creature beneath her was allowed to be a part of her life.

While they galloped along, Ricki let the reins loosen a little and stroked Diablo along the sides of his neck. It was a very tender gesture, and the horse sensed it at once. Still galloping, he raised his head, whinnied loudly, and then fell into a fast trot before Ricki even had to guide him.

It still works, she realized happily. Diablo seemed to guess what she was thinking and reacted immediately.

"You are the most intelligent horse in the world," she said breathlessly, and then gradually slowed Diablo down until they stopped, in order to wait for her friends, who were behind her.

"Man, you'd think Diablo used to run races, the way he flies. Jeepers, he's really fast! Holli is really slow in comparison," said Lillian, trying to catch her breath.

14

"There's nothing better than a good gallop," Kevin said, all traces of crabbiness gone. Cathy remarked: "I think I'm more exhausted from riding than Rashid is from running."

"Maybe you should switch roles. You buckle the saddle around you and Rashid can—"

"Yeah, right," replied Cathy with sarcasm. She turned and looked back over the path they had covered. "It's unbelievable how quickly one can go from one place to another on horseback," she said. "Just imagine how much time it would have taken us to go the same distance on foot or bicycle!"

As the four friends rode on in a slower trot, each was lost in his or her own thoughts.

Ricki arched her head back and looked up at the tops of the trees. She knew that a rider should have her eyes everywhere in order to avoid accidents, but she always loved to look up at they sky when she was riding Diablo, especially when he put one hoof in front of the other, almost like a sleepwalker, as he was right now.

Ricki could have gone on riding like this forever. The gentle sway caused by Diablo's back almost put her to sleep, and the silence of the other riders didn't help.

"Well, I'm not sure I'm going to go looking for ammonites today," she said lazily. "I'm so tired all of a sudden; I could just fall over and go to sleep."

"You must have worked too hard yesterday afternoon." Lillian looked over her shoulder back at her girlfriend and grinned, while Ricki just wrinkled her forehead, confused.

"What do you mean, I worked too hard? I don't understand… But now that we're talking about yesterday, why didn't you ask me if I wanted to go to the movies with you? I waited for you guys all afternoon and was bored to death, while you were all at the movies, stuffing your faces with popcorn and having a blast!"

Cathy looked back and forth between Kevin and Lillian with huge eyes.

"Were we at the movies?"

"Not that I know of!" the older girl replied and smiled at Ricki sympathetically. "Poor thing! You must have been in the sun too long yesterday!"

"Nonsense," said Cathy. "It was the dust in her room that settled in her brain after the big cleaning day."

"Hey, I don't get it. What's going on? Why are you two talking about my room? Don't you like it the way it is? And what do you mean about cleaning and stuff? I really did lie in the sun and—"

"See!"

"Now, just stop it! I went sunbathing and waited for you guys to come. After all, we had agreed that you would all come over right after lunch."

Ricki, standing now with her hands on her hips, looked sternly from one to the other, but all three of them were laughing.

"Don't make such a big deal out of it. Our mothers made us clean our rooms, too, and we just—"

"I didn't have to clean my room! I didn't have to do anything!"

"But Harry called and—"

"Excuse me?" Ricki slowly began to understand. "Harry! That little brat! Just wait until I get my hands on him! Now I see why he kept avoiding me yesterday. He probably wanted to get even because I had refused to give him a riding lesson on Chico. It looks like he called you all up and told you some nonsense about me having to clean my room."

16

"Right."

Kevin shook his head in admiration of Ricki's younger brother. "Pretty clever, that kid," he said. "You can see how serious he is about learning to ride."

"Serious or not, he lied to all of us and I don't like that!" Ricki fumed.

"Oh, c'mon, Ricki, don't be so mean. It's not like *you* wouldn't have done anything to be able to ride," Lillian said, trying to smooth things over. Cathy put in her reminder for a truce: "Nobody got hurt, did they?"

"Well, I think if we were to finally teach him to ride, he wouldn't need to do such things," said Kevin with reasonable practicality.

"But he deserves to be taught a little lesson," a smug grin appeared on Ricki's lips. "We'll see, maybe I'll think of something interesting!"

In the meantime, the four had approached the old weathered barn that was situated between Tom Anderson's fields. To get to this point, Ricki, her friends, and Josh, who was coming from the opposite direction, all had about the same distance to ride.

The young man was already waiting with Cherish and waved hello with his Stetson as Lillian and the others exited the woods and rode toward him.

"You have yourself a very punctual boyfriend," nodded Kevin approvingly, and Lillian answered promptly: "Well, if you got it, you got it! I'd rather have a punctual friend than an enemy who is always late."

Ricki looked baffled. "Where did you get that?"

Lillian shrugged. "I just made it up."

"That's what it sounded like! Hey, Josh, have you been waiting long?"

Lillian's boyfriend shook his head no and trotted toward them.

"No, I haven't been here long. Hi, by the way." Then he stopped Cherish right next to Doc Holliday and leaned over to Lillian with a smile.

"Hi, little one," he said softly. "Are you okay?" He gave her a kiss hello on the cheek, which made her blush. Lillian looked at her friends a little embarrassed.

Kevin laughed. "A good idea! A very good idea," he said and leaned over to Ricki.

"Hey, what about me?" asked Cathy, pretending to be insulted.

"The sun kisses you!"

"Great! Not exactly what I had in mind, but after everyone has kissed everyone, maybe we could go on riding."

"You aren't jealous, are you?" Josh teased Cathy, but she just waved him away.

"As long as no one tries to take Rashid from me, I don't have a problem."

The five riders started to trot away, heading for the old quarry where Josh had found the ammonite. Everyone was in a good mood, enjoying the day and one another's company.

"Strange," said Ricki. "We ride to the quarry so often, but we've never found any petrified objects."

"It's impossible to see them from a horse's back," replied Josh as they passed by the gate to the abandoned quarry. He jumped down and loosened the girth. Cherish took a deep breath and shook herself with pleasure.

"Get down, and then I'll show you where I found it. Maybe we'll be lucky and find some more."

"That would be fantastic," said Kevin, dismounting. "Petrified objects are really fascinating."

18

Ricki stole a sideward glance at her boyfriend and was glad she was close enough to hear him say that. Now she knew what she could give him for his birthday, which was coming up soon. A book about fossils! Perfect!

She ran merrily after the others and led Diablo carefully over the sharp stones near the entrance to the quarry.

After Josh had found the place and all five of them had walked around with their eyes on the ground for about a half hour without any luck, Ricki decided to take Diablo and leave the group for a while.

"Listen, I'm going to take Diablo out on the meadow. I saw a big tree out there with a lot of shade," she shouted to the others and left the stony area.

When she reached the shade tree a few minutes later, she sighed and sat down, leaning her back against the tree trunk.

Diablo stood in front of her and began almost immediately to doze. Every few minutes he shook his beautiful head to get rid of the bothersome flies, but his head sank lower and lower from one minute to the next.

Ricki reached out and clasped her hands around the noble head of her horse. Diablo breathed deeply and rested his head heavily on Ricki's arm.

Her heart began to beat faster from happiness. Ricki laid her forehead against the white star that was just visible under the long lock of mane on Diablo's forehead.

"You sweetheart," she whispered to him. "Do you know what a wonderful being you are? You are really something special…unique, indescribable. You are the most wonderful horse in the world, well, for me, anyway," she added after realizing that her friends felt the same way about their horses. "You're all fabulous," she decided. "God must have had a very good day when he created you horses." She pulled her horse's head even closer. And even though she began to sweat profusely in the heat, she still enjoyed every warm breath from Diablo's nostrils that wet her arm.

In that moment, as she bonded with this wonderful horse, she sensed that Diablo loved her as much as she loved him. Theirs was a very special relationship, an almost spiritual union, in which just a glance was enough to know what the other one was thinking or feeling.

"Well, either Diablo was a person in his former life or Ricki was a horse," Carlotta Mancini had said once, after she had watched Ricki and Diablo together for a while. "I have seldom seen such one-hundred percent harmony between horse and rider," and Carlotta had seen many riders with their animals.

While lost in thought with her Diablo, Ricki remembered Carlotta's remark and felt proud of the circus performer's observation. Deep down, Ricki knew that she could never have the same relationship with any other horse that she had with Diablo. He had become like a part of her.

"Nothing!" shouted Cathy loudly, and tore Ricki away from her reverie. "We didn't find a thing!"

She jerked in surprise, and even Diablo pulled his head up abruptly and stared at Cathy accusingly. She looked back at him.

"It's okay," she laughed and stroked him over his nose. "I'm sorry. I didn't want to disturb your little tête-à-tête."

Ricki stood up, yawned heartily, and stretched out her stiff arms.

"It's unbelievable how heavy a horse's head is," she said before she checked the girth. Then she got up on the saddle to rejoin her friends.

"It would have been so cool to find one," said Kevin, a little disappointed. In his mind, he had already placed an ammonite on the shelf in his room.

"By the way, I didn't bring the fossil with me," said Josh, and Kevin's face got even longer. "The next time you come to town, stop by and I'll show it to you."

Together the five rode on, over a mowed meadow. The horses trotted next to one another very mannerly, and were glad to be going toward home slowly. The cool stalls would free them from the bothersome flies that kept landing on their sweaty coats and wouldn't leave them alone.

Chapter 2

Kevin raced into the stable waving a large envelope. "You'll never believe this! Guess what I have here!"

"Not a clue. And hi, by the way," replied Ricki, who was sitting on a bale of hay with Lillian and Cathy, nibbling on a granola bar.

"Oh, come on! What do you think is in here?" Kevin looked at each of the girls, hardly able to hide his excitement.

"Well, it's probably not a bill; he wouldn't be so excited," guessed Cathy, but Lillian suddenly shot out her hand and tore the envelope out of Kevin's grasp.

"Hey, you're supposed to guess!"

"We're not playing Twenty Questions here. Wait, I'll read it out loud." Lillian took what looked like a letter out of the envelope, unfolded it, and began to read loudly and clearly:

"Darling Kevin! I have been watching you for a long time in the school yard and I would like to—"

"What? Give that to me!" Ricki grabbed for the letter. "Who would write that? So, once more: 'Dear Kevin, as you probably remember, you—' Excuse me, there's nothing here about the school yard. Lillian, you're such an idiot!"

Her girlfriend laughed.

"And you are jealous! I finally tricked you into admitting it!"

"Could you please continue reading?" asked Kevin, more than a little impatient.

"Yes! So, where was I? Oh, yes. 'As you probably remember, you participated in our contest two months ago. We are delighted to inform you that you are one of the main prizewinners. Unfortunately, you didn't win the grand prize—the weeklong riding vacation on the island of Aruba—but we are certain that you will be happy to know that you have won a three-day vacation at Stony Ridge Riding Ranch in the beautiful Appalachians Mountains. Dixie, a gelding, is waiting for you there, and you can take riding lessons on him and enjoy going for rides in the beautiful countryside. And best of all, you can bring a friend with you, so that these three days will be truly memorable. Congratulations!'"

Ricki let the letter sink down to her lap and looked at Kevin in disbelief. He was beaming.

"Well, what do you all say now?"

"Nothing!" Cathy shook her head at the incredible news, and Lillian clapped Kevin on the shoulder.

"Hey, you always were my best friend. Who are you going to take with you?"

Kevin grinned. "For sure, not you. I'd have big problems with Josh. Ricki?"

She was still holding the prize-announcement letter in her hand. "I don't know. I'd have to think about it," she said, while she looked at Diablo. She couldn't imagine being away from him for three days.

"Oh, come on, don't be a drag. I'll talk to your parents, okay?"

"Do I have a little time to think about it?" she asked.

"Okay, but I have to know by the weekend. The contest people need an answer from me."

Ricki nodded and gave him back the letter.

"Are we going riding or are we dreaming of Dixie?" joked Lillian.

"I'd rather go riding, while the weather is good. We can dream later, can't we?" Cathy jumped off the bale and ran to Rashid's stall.

"Exactly," agreed Ricki and got up as well.

"To be honest, I had enough of those flies on the ride yesterday," said Kevin. Ricki stared at him with wide eyes.

"What? Since when do you let a few mosquitoes keep you from riding? That's really something new."

"Well," stammered Kevin. "Actually, I thought maybe I'd go to town."

"Oh! The call of the ammonite! Now I see!" Lillian turned to Kevin's horse. "Sharazan, you should get yourself petrified, maybe then Kevin would pay attention to you!"

"That's ridiculous," mumbled Kevin.

"Well, I don't feel like doing anything strenuous like riding into town," explained Ricki. "What about you two?" she asked, glancing at her girlfriends. Lillian and Cathy didn't feel like bike riding just then either.

"Hey, look out the window!" called Cathy from Rashid's stall. "I think we can forget about riding. It looks like a bad storm is brewing. The sky's a very funny color."

Lillian, Ricki, and Kevin ran to the stable door and looked around.

"I think we should stay home," said Ricki, who was never very brave when it came to thunderstorms.

Lillian nodded in agreement, but Kevin made a hasty good-bye.

"I'll be in town before it even starts to rain," he said. He gave Ricki a quick kiss on the cheek and ran off. "I'll go straight home after Josh's. Don't worry about me if I don't come back today," he called, then he jumped on his bike and started pedaling furiously, trying to beat the storm.

The three girls decided to hang out in Ricki's room. There would be enough to talk about, what with Kevin's prize, to fill the whole afternoon. However, a little while later, having exhausting that subject, they began to leaf through Ricki's photo album, which was filled with pictures of her and her friends and the horses they rode.

With lots giggling and cries of "Oh, wow! Remember when we took this picture?" and "Man, that was so funny!" they burrowed themselves into their riding past and completely forgot the time.

* * *

"Come on, Kev, tell us a funny story from your youth…maybe I'll feel better then." Lillian was leaning on Doc Holliday's stall and rubbing her knee, which she had just bumped on the edge of the door.

Kevin took the piece of hay out of his mouth and smiled. "What would you like to hear?"

Lillian shrugged her shoulders.

"Maybe you could tell us about yesterday. Did you finally get to see the ammonite?"

Kevin nodded enthusiastically. "Yes! What an amazing thing, let me tell you. It was at least seven inches across."

But Lillian wasn't interested in hearing about the fossil.

25

"Did Josh say anything?" she wanted to know. Kevin shook his head.

"Your boyfriend wasn't home. But Melanie, his cousin who is visiting, showed me the stone."

Kevin's eyes were shining, and Ricki, feeling just a little insecure, wasn't sure if that shine in his eyes was because of the stone or because of Josh's cousin, but she didn't have time to think about it. Cathy looked out of the stable window and called happily, "Hey, Carlotta is on her way here!"

The teenagers left the stable in a hurry, looking forward to seeing their eccentric older friend. Even in the distance, they could see a large cloud of dust following her car. They looked at each other and grinned; all had the same thought: *How long will Carlotta's car be able to withstand her driving like a bat out of you-know-where?* Just then, the former equestrienne zoomed up the drive to the Sulais' farmhouse and came to a screeching halt on the gravel.

"Hello, Carlotta! How's your car holding up?" asked Kevin, while she awkwardly got out of the driver's seat. They were used to seeing her on her crutches, which she needed to help her walk since the circus accident many years before that maimed her and killed her horse.

"Hello, my dears. How typical of you, Kevin, asking about my car, and not wasting any words on me." Carlotta laughed and her eyes twinkled with merriment.

"Well, the way you drive, you must be feeling okay," Kevin teased, and stepped back a bit, out of the range of the crutches. He knew Carlotta would try to swipe him on the backside with them.

"Hey, did you all see that? That was attempted assault and battery on a juvenile!" Kevin teased and Ricki countered:

"Juvenile backside. I don't think there's any mention of that in the law."

Cathy jumped in. "Carlotta, we have something to tell you. Kevin won—"

"Just let me get settled here first," begged Carlotta and limped toward the stable. Before she did anything else, she had to see Rashid.

She always said, "When someone owns an animal he has to realize that it must be his first priority. These creatures are dependent on us for everything."

Rashid was already waiting for her when she reached his stall. He seemed to have an inner clock that told him Carlotta was coming, because he always raised his head over the edge of the stall at the same time every day and listened for the sound of her car. As soon as he heard the door slam shut, he whinnied to her. He knew she would visit him every day. On those few days when Carlotta couldn't manage to come to the stable, Cathy tried to comfort the animal as best she could, but he didn't really seem happy until he heard Carlotta's voice echoing through the stable, "Well, how is my favorite horse in the world?"

After she had greeted him long enough to comfort him, she turned around and looked into the faces of the four friends, who were bursting with excitement.

"Now, what's so important?" she asked.

Kevin exploded with the news.

"I won a three-day riding vacation at a dude ranch! Ricki can come with me, if she wants."

"How nice," responded Carlotta blandly, glancing over at Sharazan. "Are you taking him along?"

Kevin laughed. "No, I don't think the magazine would

27

pay for that as well. The cost of full room and board for me and Ricki is probably enough for them."

"I haven't said yet that I will go," Ricki reminded him, but Kevin was sure that his girlfriend would accompany him.

"Diablo will survive without you for a few days," he said happily, delighting in the prospect of a riding vacation, but Carlotta shook her head.

"If you have an animal, you can't shirk your responsibility for him just for your own pleasures," she said solemnly.

A look of concern crossed Kevin's face. "I don't want to neglect my responsibility, but does that mean that if you have an animal you can't go away for even a few days? After all, we couldn't ask for a better caregiver than Jake."

"That's true, but just imagine if something bad were to happen to Sharazan or Diablo while you were away. Would you want to burden Jake with that?"

"What could happen?" asked Kevin, who was beginning to feel that all this talk was spoiling his excitement of winning.

"Things happen faster than you think," answered Carlotta. "Nevertheless, it's great that you won," she said kindly. With a good-bye stroking of Rashid's nose, she left the stable and walked slowly back to her car. Just before she got in, she turned toward the four once again.

"Hey, would you like me to show you how I used to work with the horses in the circus? Sharazan and Rashid haven't forgotten anything yet."

"Wow, that would be super," shouted Cathy, who was always ready to be excited about anything that had to do with "her" Rashid.

"Well, I don't think I have anything else to do on Sunday as yet," said Carlotta, settling herself into the driver's seat.

With a final wave, she drove home, surprisingly much more slowly than she had come.

The friends exchanged glances, excited about the private circus performance but also a little pensive. Carlotta's words about possible problems had sounded like a bad omen. But they forgot about it quickly enough when Cathy said:

"Come on, let's take our darlings down to the paddock for a while."

"I'll second that!" said Ricki, and they all walked back to the stable. The animals were looking over their stalls with curiosity, and the four friends grabbed their lead ropes.

On the way to the paddock, Ricki, with an odd look on her face, observed Kevin, who was walking ahead of her with Sharazan.

"Hey, what's wrong?" asked Lillian, who caught Ricki's expression.

"I have a really funny feeling in the pit of my stomach," said Ricki softly. "Don't ask me why…that Melanie."

Lillian understood immediately.

"Jealous?" she asked, and Ricki sighed.

"I don't know. Maybe. I'm probably just being paranoid now," she tried to reassure herself.

"What do you mean, now? You're crazy all the time!" Lillian said, trying to lighten the mood.

"Thanks!"

"You're welcome, glad to help. Would you like a little more information about yourself?" Lillian asked innocently.

"No thanks, I think that will be enough for now! Want to get some ice cream after our ride?" she asked then, slightly louder.

29

"Sure, if you're buying," eagerly replied Kevin, who was, it seemed, chronically broke and always interested in ice cream.

Ricki lay in bed that night unable to fall asleep. She couldn't stop thinking that Kevin might be interested in another girl. Just the idea that she could lose Kevin caused a lump in her throat.

Maybe I'm just imagining it and being ridiculous, she thought, and pulled the blanket over her head. *But I've got to get a look at this girl Melanie.*

Before Ricki finally fell asleep, she set her clock radio for 6 a.m. Minutes before, she had decided to ride Diablo back to the quarry early in the morning. Maybe she would be lucky and find an ammonite. That would be the best present for Kevin's birthday, which was coming up on the weekend.

When the radio buzzed on at 6 a.m., it was already light, and the sunshine promised that it would be a wonderful day. In a flash, Ricki was dressed, had saddled Diablo, and both were on their way to the quarry.

Ricki knew that in two and a half hours it would be very warm, and the annoying horseflies, even at that early hour, would be landing on the horse's sweaty coat in order to sting him. She remembered with horror that she had gotten stung a few times recently as she had ridden between the fields. Hoping to avoid the flies was why she had decided to leave the house so early. She calculated that she would need about half an hour for each way—there and back. Then, theoretically, she would have about one and a half hours to search for an ammonite.

"I hope we're lucky," she said to her horse, who was trotting swiftly in the cool morning air.

They rode past the Bates farm, where they could already hear the monotonous hum of the milking machines. Ricki smiled to herself. While Dave and Margaret Bates had been working in the cow barn for almost an hour, their daughter Lillian was still asleep in her bed.

Ricki considered for a moment throwing little stones at the window of her friend's bedroom in order to get her out of bed on such a beautiful day, but she changed her mind and kept riding straight ahead. She knew if she stopped to talk with Lillian that would be the end of her search for ammonites. The two girls never talked for less than 45 minutes.

Diablo was trotting along the edge of a meadow that had already been mowed and stepped aside to avoid a mole hill. There was a whole row of them at the edge of the grass. Afterward, they trotted quickly through the small woods. From there it would take only about five minutes more for Ricki and her horse to reach the quarry.

Single rays of sunshine shot through the dense pine trees, illuminating the early morning fog, and made the atmosphere seem almost mysterious. The birds trilled loudly throughout the woods and Ricki had the feeling that she was in a fairytale land.

I should get up this early more often and ride here with Diablo, she thought, but she knew she wouldn't be able to overcome her summer vacation laziness very often. She stayed in bed till 9 a.m. most mornings with no problem.

But today she enjoyed the quiet ride alone through the woods. As much as she loved riding with her friends, being alone with Diablo in a wide-open area was like a precious gift for Ricki.

Speaking of gifts! Ammonites! Ricki stopped dreaming and urged Diablo into a slow gallop. After all, she had left so early so she could look for the stones.

Within a few minutes she had arrived at the quarry. She stopped Diablo at the barrier across the entrance and jumped down from the saddle.

Feeling in a great mood and optimistic about her search, Ricki hummed a tune as she patted Diablo on his neck. She fished a narrow little halter out of her pocket and slipped it onto the horse, after she removed the bit. Then she tied Diablo to the barrier and loosened the girth. After checking the knot on the lead, she slipped under the barrier.

"All right, my darling, I'm going to leave you by yourself for a while. Cross your hooves that I find a prehistoric stone for Kevin," said Ricki, and ran backward, away from Diablo, so that she could observe how he was taking her departure. The horse watched her for a few minutes and then began to graze. With a sigh of relief, Ricki turned around and began a step-by-step search around the site of Josh's find.

She walked relentlessly while staring at the ground. After 20 minutes, her back began to ache from walking in such a crouched position, but she bravely continued hunting.

As the sun rose higher and the morning got hotter, Ricki, who had forgotten to bring a hat to protect her from the sun, began to sweat uncomfortably and decided to stop searching, although she was disappointed. What a shame; she would have liked so much to have given Kevin an ammonite for his birthday. Oh well, she'd just have to ask her mother for a small advance on her allowance so she could buy him a book about fossils.

Ricki sighed and stretched her tense back. At the same time, she glanced toward Diablo to tell him that they would now be going home.

For a second her mouth stayed open, then she blanched and screamed, "Oh, God, no!"

"Diablo!" she yelled and ran toward the spot she had tied him up. There was no sign of her horse anywhere.

She stood in front of the barrier not knowing what to do. The halter still hung down from the pole. Diablo must have been able to slip it off somehow and was probably on his way to a more suitable grazing place.

Her hands shaking, Ricki untied the thin rope and put it back in her pocket, along with the halter. She picked up the snaffle that she had left at the barrier and ran a few yards straight ahead. She looked all around, listening closely to see if she could hear any sounds from her horse. But there was total silence.

Ricki stood still, in complete shock and visibly upset. She turned around in all directions several times. She had absolutely no idea in which direction she should go to look for Diablo.

"DIABLO! DIABLO! Don't do this!" she yelled into the silence. "You just can't do this to me! Come back! I don't feel like playing hide-and-seek! Do you hear me? DIABLO! Sweetheart, please come back!"

Ricki screamed as loud as she could but her voice soon became hoarse, and she was unable to say anything more in a normal voice. Her vocal chords were irritated and all she could do was squeak.

"Why doesn't he come back?" Ricki asked herself on the verge of tears, her heart beating wildly in her chest. "He always comes when I call him at the paddock. Why did I tie him up? Why didn't I keep an eye on him? Stupid ammonite! What am I going to do?"

Ricki knew that Diablo would use his freedom to run wild. How often did a horse have the chance to do that? There was always a fence or a stall around them. Even when they went riding cross-country, they had to follow the instructions of their riders.

"I hope at least you have fun," croaked Ricki hoarsely, and swallowed her fears for her horse. "Please God, don't let anything happen to him. Please bring him back to me," she whispered with tears in her eyes. She felt so guilty. Then she started to move again, walking first in one direction, then in another, completely without a plan. Every few yards she stopped to call Diablo, as best as she could with her sore voice.

She stamped her feet, furious. She was angry with herself for being so careless but, even more, she was afraid.

If something happens to Diablo, I don't know what I'll do, she thought, and then she started running. The day that had begun so wonderfully had turned into a nightmare.

To his surprise, Diablo had realized, after rubbing his head on one of his forelegs, that his movements were no longer restricted. The annoying halter had suddenly fallen to the ground in front of him, and now it lay in the grass almost as a challenge.

Take advantage of this freedom and go exploring, my boy, the nylon restraint seemed to be saying. *Who knows when you'll have the opportunity again to enjoy your freedom!*

Diablo looked around first, somewhat confused, and was surprised that he could turn his neck as far as he wanted.

Cautiously he took a few steps to the side until he could look in the direction of his rider. She didn't seem to notice him.

If Ricki's voice wasn't holding him back, he thought, then she must not have any objections to his looking around the area a little. The horse turned around and slowly walked away from the quarry entrance, where Ricki had tied him up.

Diablo knew that there was a fresh meadow right behind the woods they had recently ridden through, and that there he would find many herbs he loved to eat. Ricki rarely allowed him to lower his head during a ride so that he could enjoy these treats. But today he was going to eat his fill. What a terrific day this was turning out to be for him!

He ran straight for the woods so he could get to the verdant meadow as quickly as possible. Surely, Ricki wouldn't miss him.

He picked up speed in anticipation of all the delicious herbs he would soon be able to eat. After a few yards, he felt the saddle on his back slid a little to the side, and after two or three paces, it turned around completely onto his belly, where it hung uncomfortably.

Diablo stopped in surprise and turned his head around in order to see what was bothering him.

What was this? It was very strange. Now that the girth was loose, the saddle on his back, which he hardly ever felt, was jogging back and forth under his belly, and the stirrups were hanging down and bumping into his legs each time he took a step.

The animal became increasingly agitated. Where was Ricki? Why wasn't she helping him to get rid of this thing?

Diablo struck the saddle with his hind legs. When it remained in place, he started to panic. He couldn't get rid of this unpleasant thing hanging under his belly by himself. Furiously he began to buck and rear, while the saddle slid along his flanks and began to irritate the inside of his hind leg. Diablo whinnied in pain and galloped away blindly, in the hope of getting rid of this menace. He raced through the woods without looking where he was stepping. The only thing that kept him going was the desire to be free of the continuous beating against his sensitive legs.

White foam wet his coat as he continued to run. He galloped into a clearing where the small pine seedlings, which grew so close together, were hardly any higher than his withers.

The densely growing seedlings whipped against the body of the frightened horse, who was not able to understand his situation.

Suddenly Diablo screamed. He had stepped on an overgrown mossy tree stump. His hoof struck hard and then slid sideways from the wet wood. As he tried to regain his balance, his right foreleg bent under him, and the black horse fell to the ground.

For a moment he remained on the ground and waited, but then, struggling, he finally got back up on his legs. Trembling, Diablo tried to take one step at a time, but the pain in his leg was so intense that he had no choice but to accept his fate and stand still. The saddle was still hanging below his belly, and by now it looked pretty banged up. One of the stirrups had torn off and the leather of the seat had deep tears in it.

Diablo held his painful leg at an angle and panted from the strain. Where was Ricki? Why didn't she come to help him, to free him from this terrible leather thing and to comfort him, to take away his fear, to stroke him calmly, and to talk to him.

Slowly he raised his magnificent head. The veins were so swollen, they looked as though they would burst. Diablo whinnied weakly in the hope that his best friend would hear him.

Chapter 3

Jake had been finished with his stable chores for quite a while and was now pacing back and forth nervously in front of the stalls.

He kept glancing at the large round clock that Ricki had installed above the tack room doorway.

"Where can she be so long?" he asked himself for the umpteenth time within the last 15 minutes. It was now after 10 a.m., and he knew from talking to Brigitte that Ricki had left the house just after 6 a.m., because she had heard the door close about that time.

Lupo, the stable tomcat was winding around Jake's feet, purring, but today, unlike other days, the old man hardly paid him any attention. He watched the bundle of tiger-striped fur at his feet, but was so deep in thought he never once bent down to pet him. He was much too worried about Ricki, who rarely rode out in the morning and, when she did, she never stayed out so long.

The cat tried once more to get Jake's attention, but he soon realized that wasn't going to happen just now, and he withdrew, sulking, to Chico's stall, where he curled up cozily in the little donkey's feed trough. Chico was glad for the unexpected visit. He stroked his soft muzzle gently over Lupo's fur and the tomcat immediately began to purr. In less than a minute, he had fallen asleep.

"Isn't she back yet?" asked Brigitte Sulai, who had come running over to the stable when she saw Jake standing in the doorway.

The old man shook his head no.

"Do you think something has happened to her?" Ricki's mother looked very concerned and stared out over the neighboring fields.

"Diablo is a pretty sure-footed horse," Jake replied, avoiding a definite answer. He didn't want to worry Brigitte any more than she already was. He knew that even when there was no problem, she worried when it came to horses and riding.

"But you're worried, too," Brigitte noticed. "Admit it. Ricki should have been home ages ago, shouldn't she?"

Jake sighed. "Not necessarily. It depends. We don't know who she ran into while she was out. She sometimes forgets all about the time."

"No excuses, Jake!"

The old man turned away. He couldn't explain Ricki's being gone so long any better than Brigitte could.

"I'm sure she'll be here in the next half hour," he mumbled into his chin, and reached for the broom so that he could sweep the stable corridor for the third time. He just couldn't stand around doing nothing.

"Well, I don't want to depend on that. I think I should have Marcus start looking for her with the car." Brigitte turned around and was about to return to the house when Jake called after her:

"Where is Marcus supposed to look for her? We don't even know where she rode off to."

Ricki's mother stopped dead in her tracks.

"That's right! Ooh, I'm as mad as a hornet! Just wait until she gets home. At least she could have left us a note telling us where she was heading. Then we'd know where to look!" Brigitte didn't know whether she should be frightened or angry, but at that moment she was probably feeling both. She walked back to the house, her hands clenched, while Jake threw the broom into the corner.

"Darn it!" he said, grinding his teeth. "Come home!"

Ricky had searched for Diablo in every direction around the quarry, but she still had not found his tracks.

With trembling knees, she decided to go home. Maybe Diablo had come to the same conclusion, too, and was already in the paddock or in his stall, happy as a clam. And if not, well, she didn't even want to think about "if not." At least, when she got home, she could round up a few people to help her look for Diablo.

Ricki ran as fast as she could across the meadow and toward the woods, which she needed to pass through to get home.

In the midmorning sun, Ricki could already feel the impending intense heat of the day. Her T-shirt was soaking wet, and by the time she reached the shade of the trees, she was physically and emotionally exhausted.

She allowed herself a brief rest, leaning her back against one of the tree trunks. But for the moment, she couldn't go on, and she sunk to a sitting position, clasped her arms around her knees, and let her head sink down to them. She closed her eyes, completely drained of her strength. Her heart was aching and her legs didn't seem to work any-more, but the worst thing was not knowing where Diablo was, and whether he would survive this unscathed.

"Never again," Ricki swore to herself. "I'll never tie up Diablo again and go away and leave him. I'm an idiot, I should have known better. I just hope nothing has happened to him! I would never, ever forgive myself! Oh, God, Jake is going to kill me when he finds out. *His* Diablo..." Ricki couldn't calm down, she was so overwhelmed with guilt.

Suddenly she jerked her head up. What was that? Had she actually heard a faint whinnying in the distance or had she just imagined it?

She got up slowly and listened intently into the silence of the woods.

There! Again!

Ricki's heart leaped.

"DIABLO!" she shouted. "DIABLO! Where are you?"

She heard the soft whinnies again, and this time she was sure it was her own black horse.

She took a deep breath and, with her last ounce of ener-gy, spurted in the direction of the sound.

"Hi, Jake, what's happening?" In a good mood, Lillian sauntered into the stable and threw a bag of day-old dry bread into the corner. "The others will be here in a minute. We decided to polish our saddles today. It's too hot to ride anyway."

The elderly man glanced at the plastic bag with disap-proval. Some of the contents had spilled out onto the floor.

"Perhaps you noticed that the floor had already been swept!" he said with irritation. "You kids always throw your things all over the stable and I have to clean it up!"

41

Lillian, who was cuddling with her Doc Holliday, turned to Jake in surprise.

"I hope you're having a nice day, too, dear Jake! What's wrong? Why are you in such a bad mood on such a nice day? You'd think that—"

"Ricki's gone."

"What?" Lillian wasn't sure she heard him right.

"Ricki and Diablo are gone, somewhere out in the area."

"So what? We go riding almost every day, isn't that true?" Lillian wrinkled her forehead. What was wrong with Jake? Why was he so uptight about Ricki riding off on Diablo?

"They've been gone since about 6 a.m. this morning! And it's already after 11 a.m.! Do you understand now why I'm upset?!"

"Since 6 a.m.? She must be made of leather!"

"We don't even know where she rode off to. At any rate, I have a bad feeling."

"We'll have to—" Lillian started to laugh, but when she saw how worried Jake was, she became serious at once.

"Is something… I mean, did something happen to her?"

Just then Cathy and Kevin breezed in.

"Hi, you all, how's it going? Hey, Lil, have you separated the saddles yet? Hey, Jake. Say, what's the matter with you? Haven't you eaten yet?" Cathy giggled over her own joke.

Just as Kevin took a breath to add his own comments, Jake walked away without saying a word.

"What's his problem?" Kevin asked. "Am I wrong, or did he look stressed out?"

Lillian walked toward her friends, her face drawn and her lips tense.

"Ricki has disappeared with Diablo," she said solemnly.
"What?"

"That's a stupid joke! *Really?*"

Lillian shook her head forcefully.

"It's no joke—honestly! She rode off about 6 a.m. this morning and—"

"Six o'clock?" groaned Cathy. "Is that girl crazy? That's still nighttime!"

"Can you just listen?" Two pairs of eyes fixed on Lillian. "Good. Well, Ricky left that early this morning, told no one where she was going, and hasn't come back yet. It's been…" she looked at the clock on the wall, "over five hours, if I added it up right."

"Oh," said Kevin.

"Is that all you can think of to say?" asked Lillian, while Cathy, who had turned pale, leaned against the stable wall.

"Do you think something has happened?" she asked softly.

"I have no idea," answered Lillian, lowering her gaze. "Maybe we should put off cleaning the saddles and start looking for Ricki and Diablo."

"With the horses?" asked Kevin, and looked dubiously at the sky, which was bright blue with a blazing sun.

"It's too hot!" responded Lillian. "Let's ride our bikes instead."

"Good," agreed Cathy. "I'll run over to the house and tell Ricki's mother that we're going. She'll feel better when she knows that we're out looking for Ricki." And with that, she ran off.

Less than five minutes later, the friends were on the path that lead to the road.

"Where are we going?" asked Kevin while he pedaled furiously.

"Hmm, to tell the truth, I have no idea where they could be," admitted Cathy, who had to stop her bike in order to avoid running into Lillian, who had stopped with no warning and jumped out of the saddle.

"Hey! Are you crazy?" yelled Cathy, but the older girl didn't pay any attention to her.

"I have an idea where she could be," murmured Lillian secretively.

"Well, don't keep us in suspense, tell us," Kevin looked at her, the tension visible in his whole body.

"I think she rode to the quarry," the older girl said.

"What? Why should she?" Kevin was baffled.

"Because of you, you dimwit! Don't you get it?"

"No, honestly, I don't!"

"Your birthday is in two days, isn't it? And what do you want the most? An ammonite! And where can these things be found, maybe? At the quarry! And who wants to get you something special? Ricki!"

Now Cathy and Kevin understood.

"Exactly," said Cathy. "You're right."

Kevin, however, was very quiet. If something happened to Ricki just because she had wanted to get him his wish, he would never get over it. *She must really love me!* he thought in amazement.

"Don't just stand there dreaming!" scolded Lillian. "We've got to get going. After all, it's a pretty good distance from here."

The three of them jumped back onto their bikes and raced through the noontime heat.

Ricki had to stop every once in a while. Her breath was labored and she was starting to see little stars before her eyes due to her exertions in the heat. Panting, she pressed her hands into her left side, where she felt a sharp pain. Ricki hoped she was going in the right direction. She hadn't heard any whinnying for quite a while.

She asked herself again if the sounds had just been her imagination.

He has to be here, she tried to convince herself. With that thought foremost in her mind, she forced herself to keep going.

The perspiration that ran into her eyes made them burn and hampered her sight.

"DIABLO!" she called yet again. "DIABLO, are you here?" and from not far away, she could hear his answer distinctly. She almost collapsed. Scared, she turned completely around and noticed a dark shape moving in the clearing on the right.

"Thank you, God!" she whispered and stumbled forward. She didn't even notice the branches that whipped into her face on the way. The only thing that mattered was seeing Diablo—one of the most important beings in her life—there in front of her. It looked like he wasn't hurt, but the fact that he didn't walk toward her, as he usually did, frightened her. Then she thought that maybe, just maybe, the saddle was caught on some underbrush, and Diablo couldn't free himself.

Ricki's legs trembled badly. She could hardly walk anymore, but she had to get closer to her beloved horse. About two yards from him, she forced herself to stop. The last thing she wanted was to spook him. Softly she called his name and began to talk to him in a soothing voice, saying all sorts of things, things she couldn't even remember saying afterward.

When she was sure he had recognized her, she slowly approached him. Diablo whinnied a reserved greeting, but he didn't move any closer to her.

"What's wrong, my darling? Come here to me. You're not mad at me, are you? I'm so sorry. Come here, please."

When Ricki was close enough, the sight she saw shocked her.

Diablo was standing on three legs. His fourth leg, which was very swollen at the pastern joint, he held at an angle. His body was crusted over with welts he had gotten from galloping through the dense trees. The saddle hung down from the rear of his belly, and was very badly damaged.

Desperate, Ricki shut her eyes for a moment. "Oh my goodness, what have I done to you?" she mumbled, swallowing the sobs that were rising in her throat.

With three more steps, she finally reached her horse and cautiously stretched out her hand to him. Diablo didn't move an inch, but he stretched his neck trustingly as far as possible toward her.

He seemed to say: *It's lucky you're finally here. What took you so long?*

Ricki threw her arms around her black horse and hugged him close. Sobbing and sniffing, she laid her face on his warm coat and breathed in his smell.

The world seemed forgotten around her. She had her cherished Diablo back again.

After a few seconds, she remembered the reality.

With trembling hands, she slipped on the snaffle, so that he couldn't run off again. Then she held the reins tightly in one hand, while she carefully felt along his belly to the girth and, with tremendous effort, undid the buckle. The saddle fell to the ground and frightened Diablo, causing him to jump to the side on three legs.

"Stay calm, boy, nothing happened. That stupid thing just fell off. Don't be afraid," Ricki said firmly, although she was shaking all over.

After the two of them had calmed down somewhat, Ricki examined the horse's pastern, which was swollen to the size of a grapefruit.

"And this is all because of me and that stupid stone!" she sobbed. But this was no time for tears of guilt. She had to get a grip on herself and think clearly. How was she going to bring Diablo home?

"Can you walk?" she asked him with sympathy, and tried to get him to take a step. Diablo exerted all his muscle strength and hopped beside Ricki on three legs.

"Well, at least we're making some progress," Ricki praised her horse and patted him on the neck.

"We'll make it, Diablo! For sure, even if it takes us days. You'll see, when we're out of the clearing, it'll get easier for you. Oh, Diablo, I'm so glad I found you again. Forgive my stupidity," she begged him, and once again she felt her eyes fill with tears as Diablo looked at her with love and trust.

Things like this happen, he seemed to say before the two of them moved on, very, very slowly.

Lillian, Cathy, and Kevin almost flew to the quarry on their bikes. Worry about Ricki and Diablo pumped up their muscles and gave them more strength.

"Come on, we'll take a shortcut," suggested Cathy. She turned into a very narrow path that was hardly visible between two cornfields.

"Are you sure this leads to the quarry?" Kevin, doubtful, shouted to Cathy, who was riding in front of him. Suddenly the path just evaporated into nothing.

"I'm sure, but we might have to push our bikes part of the way."

This "part of the way" turned out to be the length of the meadow, and it took the three teens about half an hour.

"That wasn't such a good idea! It would have been much quicker if we had taken the riding path through the woods," Lillian said, a little disgruntled.

"Yeah, I know," Cathy responded. "I just forgot that the meadow was so long. I'm really sorry."

As the three of them finally arrived at the quarry, they were disappointed not to discover either Ricki or Diablo.

"That doesn't mean anything," Lillian defended her decision. After all, it's been six hours since Ricki rode off. It's very possible she was here."

Kevin had dismounted and was looking around, but he couldn't recognize anything that would have proven Ricki had been there earlier.

"Let's go back," he said finally. "Maybe she's already home. I can't take this heat any longer."

Cathy nodded.

"But this time, let's take the direct way through the woods," decided Lillian, and jumped back on her bike.

The friends pedaled toward the woods in silence, each hoping it wouldn't take too long. A little shade would be welcome in this heat.

Sooner than they thought, they turned off into the pleasant coolness of the woods.

In order to give themselves a little rest from so much physical activity in the heat, they rode slowly in single file, all lost in their own thoughts. Then Lillian, who was in front, screamed shrilly. Startled, Kevin stopped short, causing Cathy to plow into his rear fender.

"What the—?"

"Look, up ahead! There they are! But why is Ricki walking beside Diablo? Something's wrong!"

Lillian raced ahead. Kevin and Cathy right behind her.

"Diablo is walking so strangely," Cathy observed loudly.

"Ricki, *Ric-kiii!* Wait, we'll be right there," yelled Lillian to her girlfriend, who stopped and turned around at the sound of her name.

She was so relieved when she recognized Lillian and the others. It felt good not to be alone anymore.

"Hey, how come you're riding your bikes? Aren't your horses good enough?" she tried to joke, but her pale face and painful smile told her friends that she really wasn't in a joking mood.

"What happened?" asked Kevin. He breathed a sigh of relief as he saw that Ricki seemed to be okay.

"I was stupid!" his girlfriend answered curtly. "I tied Diablo up at the quarry and then I didn't watch him after that. He must have rubbed the halter loose and taken off."

"Where's your saddle?" Cathy wanted to know. Ricky told them where she had found Diablo and the condition in which she found him.

"I left it lying there. Right now, I have to figure out how I'm going to get Diablo home. I have no idea what happened to his leg," sighed Ricki.

The four teens looked at each other for suggestions. Finally Lillian said, "I think we should split up. Cathy, ride home and tell Ricki's mother what happened. I'll see if I can find the saddle. Kevin?"

49

Kevin nodded. "I'll stay with Ricki, okay?"

Ricki smiled at Lillian with gratitude.

"You guys are terrific. Thank you so much. Maybe someday I can make it up to you," she said.

"The main thing is that Diablo recovers," Lillian responded. "Nothing else matters. So, see you later."

"Right. See you later," said Cathy, and the two girls took off, each in a different direction.

"How did you ever find us?" Ricki asked Kevin.

He said as innocently as possible: "Lillian had an idea that you would be at the quarry. She didn't say why."

Kevin looked away, hoping Ricki wouldn't notice that he told a little lie. She didn't, but shyly she admitted to him the reason for her early-morning mission.

"I wanted to look for your birthday present. I guess it wasn't meant to be!"

Kevin embraced his girlfriend and gave her a tender kiss on the cheek.

"Just the attempt alone is a wonderful present. Thanks for all your efforts," he said and smiled at her. Ricki nodded and pointed at Diablo, who was completely exhausted.

"We have to get home. He needs rest right away. And I want to call Dr. Hofer and ask him to come by and check him out."

Kevin agreed, and the two started toward home again with an injured Diablo. It would take at least two hours before they would be back at the stable.

"Should I take him for a while?" asked Kevin, sometime later. Ricki just shook her head.

"It's my fault that he can't walk well," she kept saying, and Kevin decided that it would be better not to say anything about it anymore. He put his arm around her shoulders and tried to comfort her, but Ricki didn't even seem to notice him.

"It's my fault. I just hope he didn't break anything. If I had only known, I would have stayed home, would have read or done something else. I would never have gone riding. It's my fault," Ricki babbled on, seemingly numb with guilt.

Kevin, his arm still around her shoulders, glanced secretly at his watch.

I just hope Cathy uses her head and tries to organize a rescue party with a horse trailer, he thought. He looked at Diablo, who seemed to be going more and more slowly, and then at Ricki, who retreated further into herself with each step.

Cathy, hurry up! he begged silently. *The two of them can't keep this up much longer.*

Chapter 4

Ricki stood with shaking knees in the stable corridor and held tight to Diablo's halter. They had been back home for more than an hour. Cathy had been so thoughtful. She had gone over to Lillian's parents' farm and asked Dave Bates to help out with his horse trailer.

However, getting the horse into the trailer had taken much longer that Lillian's father thought it would. It was an enormous effort for Diablo to hop three-legged into the trailer after having walked so far. It also didn't help that the metal ramp sounded frighteningly loud with every step taken and the trailer was bumped about each time the horse hopped upward, but finally Diablo had managed it.

Ricki had sat beside the horse in the trailer, although it generally was not permitted for a human to ride with the horse, for safety's sake. But she felt it was the least she could do for Diablo at the moment.

Luckily the Bates's trailer had an opening in the front, so that Diablo didn't have to back out of the trailer when they arrived home.

Brigitte embraced her daughter without a word, happy that she was back safe and sound. The scolding that she had intended was out of the question now. Even Jake patted Ricki comfortingly on the shoulder. However, she had noticed that his face became tense as he examined Diablo's swollen leg.

"Doc Hofer has to come immediately," the old man insisted, and he stroked the swollen pastern with his gnarled hand, carefully and tenderly.

Diablo jerked back. His leg must be more painful than Ricki had thought.

"Jake, I'm so sorry," she stammered. She knew that Jake's feelings for Diablo were like that of a father's for his child.

Jake sniffed noisily. "I just hope Diablo hasn't injured himself seriously," he said, very worried.

Brigitte had hurried into the house in order to phone the vet. Lillian, Cathy, and Kevin stood around in front of the stalls, feeling they were in the way, and they tried to avoid looking at Jake. They had seen him take a handkerchief out of his pocket when he thought no one was looking, in order to wipe the tears from his eyes.

After a few minutes, Brigitte came hurrying back.

"Doctor Hofer will be here soon. I reached him on his cell phone; he just happened to be close by."

"Thank God," mumbled Jake, and Ricki's heart began to beat even more rapidly than before.

Brigitte looked at her daughter with tenderness. She knew how Ricki was suffering, blaming herself for Diablo's injury. "Sweetheart, don't you want to go in the house and eat something, or should I bring you something to drink? After all, it's already 3 p.m." But Ricki just shook her head dejectedly.

"Thanks, Mom, but I can't eat anything right now…not

until I find out what's wrong with Diablo." Her friends all nodded in understanding.

Since it looked as though Ricki was not going to say anything else, and she certainly was not going to go into the house, Brigitte sighed and left the stable.

"I'll go and see if Dr. Hofer is coming," said Cathy, just to say something.

"I'll go with you," Lillian said, taking her arm. Even Kevin pushed himself away from Sharazan's stall.

He wanted to say something comforting to Ricki as he passed her, but the look in her eye told him there was nothing he could say. She was too involved in her guilt for Kevin to help her. The only thing that could help her would be a positive prognosis from Dr. Hofer.

Ricki stoked Diablo's neck rhythmically.

What's keeping the vet? she asked herself every few seconds. Diablo's neck slowly drooped with fatigue. He was just as tired as Ricki.

"He's coming!" she heard Lillian shouting out front. "Dr. Hofer is on his way! At last!"

Ricki took a deep breath. She would know soon.

The vet stood in front of Diablo and stroked his chin thoughtfully. "Hmm," he said, staring at the swollen pastern joint. "It's too swollen to make a clear diagnosis. The swelling prevents me from examining the motion of the joint. I can't even probe the tendons properly."

He turned around to Ricki, and looked at Jake as well.

"If we want to be sure, we should X-ray the leg."

"X-ray?" Ricki became even paler. "Does that mean we have to take Diablo to Dr. Lambertin's horse clinic? That's 30 miles away!"

54

"Well, I could ask a colleague to lend me a portable X-ray machine. Then we could take the pictures here in the stable," replied Dr. Hofer.

"That's probably very expensive, isn't it?" asked Ricki softly.

"Well, it's not cheap, but it won't bankrupt your family either." The vet laughed quietly.

"I have a savings account. Please, Dr. Hofer, can we carry out this examination soon? I just can't relax for a minute until I find out what's really wrong with Diablo's leg."

Dr. Hofer nodded.

"I'll speak with my colleague right away. If possible, I'll pick up the equipment today. Then I could take the X-rays this evening, at the latest. Until then, please keep the joint cool. Do you have a cooling gel bandage?"

Jake shook his head.

"No? Too bad, that would have been perfect. However, a towel soaked in cold water will work, too. You can wrap a normal bandage around it to keep it in place. Mix some aluminum acetate into the water. That can really work wonders with swelling. Change the bandage every half hour. Or you can take a cup and pour the water mixture over the bandage every half hour. The important thing is that the bandage doesn't dry out and that it cools the swelling down."

"We'll get started right away," said Jake as he shook the doctor's hand.

Ricki nodded, grateful for the information. At least she wouldn't have to stand around doing nothing.

While Dr. Hofer dialed his colleague on his cell phone in the car, Ricki was already mixing the aluminum acetate and water in a bucket. Jake found a small, thick terrycloth towel and the dark blue bandages still in their original packaging. Ricki had never needed them before.

Ricki gently laid the soaking-wet towel around Diablo's pastern joint and then even more carefully wrapped the bandage around that.

At first, Diablo was a little frightened and jerked back as the cool wetness penetrated his coat, but soon he gave a relaxed sigh. The bandage seemed to relieve him. He looked at Ricki gratefully, who was crouched in front of him checking on the bandage.

"Do you think I wrapped it too tightly?" she asked Jake, but he shook his head decidedly.

"You did everything just right. Put Diablo in his stall and go and eat something. Your horse needs peace and quiet—and so do you. I'll pour water over the bandage for the next two hours myself."

Ricki didn't dare contradict the man who had cared for Diablo since he was a colt. Although she would have preferred staying with her horse, she followed Jake's instructions.

To be honest, she was so hungry that she was almost dizzy. Up to now, she had thought the queasy feeling she had was a result of the whole upsetting experience, but now her stomach was really growling.

Gratefully, she nodded to Jake. She stroked the soft nostrils of her horse with a worried look, and then she left the stable, her tired body barely able to drag itself the short distance to the house.

"Are you coming?" she asked her friends, and they followed her immediately. "You're probably all dying of hunger, too."

"Actually, I'm dying of thirst more," said Cathy, but

then, on seeing the delicious sandwiches piled on a platter in the middle of the Sulais' kitchen table, she began to feel the emptiness in her stomach.

"Help yourselves," said Brigitte, pouring tall glasses of ice-cold homemade lemonade. She was glad Ricki's appetite seemed to have returned.

Ricki sat and reached for a sandwich. Silently and listlessly she took a bite, chewing slowly, while her friends ravenously attacked the sandwiches and talked excitedly about the X-ray examination that was going to be performed in the stable soon.

"I watched them doing that once," Lillian mumbled with her mouth full. "I don't think I'll ever understand how a machine like that works."

"The main thing is that it works," responded Cathy, and, giving Brigitte a big smile, she reached for another sandwich. They were really delicious.

"Did you find the second stirrup from Ricki's saddle?" Kevin asked Lillian.

"No, I have no idea where Diablo lost it. Say, Ricki? Do you think the saddle repair shop will be able to fix it? It looks pretty damaged."

Ricki stared at her lemonade glass.

"Ricki?"

"Oh, I'm sorry. I wasn't listening. What did you say?"

"I asked if you thought whether your saddle can be repaired. After all—"

"I don't care." Ricki cut off Lillian.

"But—"

"But, nothing! I couldn't care less about that stupid saddle! I just want Diablo to get better. I don't care about anything else!"

Cathy nodded full of sympathy.

"You're right, but, do you know something?" She made a little pause before she continued talking. "I have a gut feeling that Diablo will be well much faster than you think."

Ricki looked at her friend. Oh, how she wanted to believe her!

"Do you really think so?" she asked hopefully.

Cathy nodded energetically. "I'm sure! I feel it!"

"I just hope you're right," whispered Ricki, who was almost in tears again. As Kevin silently put his arms around her, she broke down again.

"I love Diablo so much," she sobbed, her voice breaking. Then, suddenly, she was overcome with coughing, due to a crumb that got stuck in her throat.

"Oh man," she panted, and Lillian gave her a big smile.

"If you suffocate here, the doctor will have to bring that portable machine into the kitchen to use on you. That really will be expensive, I can tell you."

"You idiot," coughed Ricki, but then she started to laugh a little.

"If she says, 'you idiot,' she must be feeling better," Cathy announced, grinning, and at once the whole tense atmosphere loosened up a bit.

Ricky held on to Cathy's premonition and imagined herself riding happily around Echo Lake again in a few weeks on Diablo.

She sighed deeply.

Yes, this picture gave her strength and new courage. Suddenly she was sure that Dr. Hofer's prognosis would be okay. With this in mind, peace returned to her heart.

Diablo would be healthy again.

It was exactly 6:30 p.m. when Dr. Hofer packed up the portable X-ray machine and put it in his van.

"I have two more appointments, and if there are no more emergencies in the meantime, I'll drive straight back to the office and develop the films. As soon as I know more, I'll call you."

He opened the small refrigerator in which he kept medicines, and took out a large tube of ointment and handed it to Ricki.

"Keep cooling that leg until you go to bed tonight. Before you close up the stable, unwrap the bandage and smear this paste thickly onto the swollen area. After about half an hour, it will get hard, like dried clay. Let it work overnight. In the morning, you can just crumble it away. Then continue with the wet bandages. I'll come by tomorrow morning and then we'll see what to do next."

Ricki nodded gratefully. She would do anything for Diablo. If it would help, she would wrap the leg day and night or massage it. The main thing was that Diablo's leg got better.

When Dr. Hofer drove off, Ricki was already beginning to feel some relief. She had noticed happily that Diablo had put his hoof back on the floor, even if carefully.

"If the leg were broken or sprained, he wouldn't put any weight on it at all," said Jake, and Ricki shared his opinion.

"Better to be safe than sorry," she said, glad that they had X-rayed Diablo and that he had allowed them to do it without making a fuss.

Now it was like sitting on pins and needles, waiting for the phone call from Dr. Hofer. During the time he spent with Diablo, the vet had received several calls: a cow that was having trouble calving, a dog that had been hit by a car. It could be a while before Ricki heard from him.

Her friends had left for home a long time ago, as Ricki unwrapped the bandage at 10 p.m. and carefully dried the hair around the area. Then she smeared the thick paste all over the pastern joint.

"Well, my darling? Are you feeling better? You know, I have the feeling that the swelling has gone down a little bit. Jake, what do you think? Am I imagining it, or is it really a little less swollen?" Ricki looked up at Jake, who was standing next to her, with hopeful and questioning eyes.

The old man bent down awkwardly to examine Diablo's leg more closely. With his eyes squinted almost shut, he carefully felt along the swollen area and slowly he began to nod.

"I think you're right," he said, and Ricki's heart jumped for joy.

"Thank God. If the X-ray is okay, I'll be able to sleep tonight," said Ricki, trying to suppress a yawn. She was dead tired after this strenuous day.

After she had brought Diablo back to his stall and given him an affectionate hug, she said good night to Jake, who carefully locked the stable door behind them and, more slowly than usual, walked across to his little cottage. It had not been an easy day for him either.

Brigitte would have liked to send Ricki right to bed, but she knew how important it was to her daughter to hear what Dr. Hofer had to say. Instead she wrapped a thick blanket around Ricki, who had snuggled up in a large armchair in the living room right beside the telephone. Ricki tried her best to stay awake, but within five minutes her eyes fell closed.

About 30 minutes later, deep in sleep, she registered the ringing of the phone but she was too zoned out to react to it.

Ricki? Ricki!" Her mother's soft voice and gentle shaking of her arm tried to wake her.

"Hmmm?" said Ricki, and blinked around at her surroundings.

"Dr. Hofer phoned. Diablo's leg is okay. Nothing broken! Come, get up and go to bed."

Ricki smiled happily.

"God, I am so glad! Thank you!" she mumbled half asleep but with relief. Then she settled down even deeper into the armchair.

Brigitte looked at her daughter lovingly. She seemed so fragile when she was sleeping. A wave of tenderness overwhelmed the mother, and she gave Ricki a kiss on her forehead.

"Sleep well, little one," she whispered and tucked the blanket in around Ricki's feet. She knew Ricki wasn't able to move one more inch tonight.

Quietly Brigitte tiptoed out of the room and turned off the light. Although Ricki's mother didn't have a close relationship with horses in general, she was glad that Diablo hadn't injured himself more seriously.

Ricki woke up and blinked a little in confusion, as she realized that she was not in her bed as usual. Slowly she stretched her muscles. The night in the armchair hadn't been very comfortable.

She yawned and then remembered what her mother had told her late last night.

DIABLO! EVERYTHING IS OKAY!

All at once Ricki was totally awake. A big grin covered her face. She was beaming as though she had won the lottery.

She quickly folded the fluffy blanket and went upstairs to take a shower and wash away the worry and grime of yesterday.

While the water was running over her body, her brain kicked into gear.

Today is Saturday, she thought. *Dr. Hofer wanted to come by this morning, Diablo needs a new bandage, and otherwise... There was something else. Darn it, I know I've forgotten something!* Ricki racked her brain, but she just couldn't seem to remember.

"Well, then it must not have been too important," she mumbled to herself while she dried her hair with a bath towel.

About 15 minutes later, she left the bathroom in a good mood and went to her room to put on fresh clothes. She was singing on her way there when she almost ran into her little brother, Harry, who had just come out of his bedroom unexpectedly.

"Hey? What's with you? Can't you watch where you're going?" Harry complained loudly.

"Shhh! Do you want to wake up Mom and Dad?" Ricki scolded him, but the little boy was not yet wide awake himself.

"Why not? It's already 8:30 a.m.!"

"Nonsense! It's a just 6:30 a.m.! So get back in bed!"

"You can't tell me what to do! You aren't my mother! Anyway, if it's that early, how come you're up already?"

"I have to bandage Diablo's leg. Dr. Hofer phoned late last night and said that nothing is broken," Ricki explained to her brother."

"Who broke a bandage?"

"Oh, Harry! Forget it! Go back to sleep!"

Quickly she nudged him back into his room, then went next door to hers and got dressed in less than five minutes.

Back in the kitchen, she took two apples from the fruit bowl and quietly left the house, headed for the stable, where Jake was already at work.

"Good morning, Jake! Diablo didn't break anything! Isn't that super?"

The old man leaned on the handle of the pitchfork.

"Morning, Ricki! Dr. Hofer called?"

Ricki nodded and her face beamed.

"I am *sooo* happy," she said, giving Jake a big, hard hug that almost took his breath away. Relief was flooding Ricki's whole being, making her euphoric. In the next instant she ran over to Diablo's stall and pushed open the sliding door.

"My sweetheart! You're going to be okay! How are you? Does it still hurt? Come, let me see if the paste from the vet did any good overni— Oh, Jake, you already changed the bandage! Thanks a lot. How did the swelling look? Did it look better?"

Jake went over to the stall and glanced in.

"I'd say that it's a little better. It doesn't seem to hurt him as much as it did yesterday. Did you notice, he put a little weight on that leg again."

While Ricki hugged the black horse's neck, she glanced down at the leg.

"That's great!" she said. But now that the worst was over, she knew she still had to face up to Jake. So she took a deep calming breath and turned to him.

63

"Are you mad at me for not taking good care of Diablo?" she asked. Jake, who looked at her for a long time, finally he shook his head.

"No, Ricki, I'm not mad at you. This time the story has a happy ending, but you know that it could have ended very differently. I think it was a good lesson for you for the future. Don't ever let your horse out of your sight and don't ever forget that you have taken over the responsibility for Diablo. You saw how fast something can happen in one careless moment."

Ricki looked down at her feet ashamed. She knew she could have prevented the whole thing if she had taken better care of him.

"That will never happen again, Jake, I swear it!" she promised.

Jake looked at her intently. "I know," he said and turned away, back to his chores.

After lunch Lillian, Cathy, and Kevin were back in the stable. One look at Ricki's relaxed face was enough to tell them that everything was going to be all right again with Diablo.

"See? I told you! I had a feeling," Cathy laughed, relieved.

Lillian raised both arms. "Do you also have a feeling about when my legs are going to stop aching? I must have strained my calf muscles yesterday by balancing the saddle on the handlebars and riding home. I don't think I can even sweep today," she groaned loudly.

"When you're stiff, moving around helps," grinned Kevin, and threw a brush at Lillian, who caught it without any problem.

"If you can do that, you can sweep," he laughed, while all Lillian could do was shrug her shoulders.

"Well, I can try, I guess," she said, and then she got Doc Holliday and led him out of his stall in order to give him a good brushing.

"What did the vet say later on last night?" Cathy wanted to know. She had started to groom her Rashid in his stall.

Ricki sat on a hay bale across the corridor from the horse's stall. "Well, nothing is broken. He gave him a shot earlier today, so that the swelling goes down faster, and I'm supposed to put on the paste every night and leave it on overnight. Of course, he has to be taken care of during the next few weeks. Dr. Hofer said I should leave him in his stall for three or four days, and then I can slowly start letting him walk, lead him about or something. At first only 15 minutes, and then a little longer every day."

"You know," said Lillian, "it's too hot outside, anyway. I suggest we leave the other horses and Chico inside as well, then Diablo won't be all alone. We can exercise the other horses in the evening, and Harry walks around with Chico all the time anyway."

Ricky smiled gratefully at her girlfriend. It would have broken her heart if the other horses had been able to gambol about in the paddock while Diablo, unable to understand why, was forced to stay in his stall longing to be outside with the others.

"That's exactly what we'll do," agreed Cathy, and Kevin nodded his approval of the idea while he combed Sharazan's long tail.

Ricki, who already had groomed her Diablo early that morning, watched her friends complete the grooming of their animals from her perch on the bale.

65

"Carlotta hasn't been here yet today," she said suddenly. "Didn't she want to show us some circus training moves with Rashid and Sharazan."

"That was tomorrow," remembered Cathy.

"Too bad what I wanted to do yesterday didn't work out," Ricky thought out loud suddenly.

"Hmmm," mused Lillian, who knew what her friend was talking about. "I guess it just wasn't meant to be."

"It wasn't good for Diablo!" said Kevin, and instantly he was sorry he had said it. He remembered that none of this wouldn't have happened if Ricki hadn't been searching for an ammonite for him.

"I know," his girlfriend answered softly, and all of a sudden she remembered what she had forgotten this morning: Tomorrow is Kevin's birthday!

"Shoot!" she said to herself. It was too late to make it into town on her bike, all of the book stores would have already closed by the time she got there. It looked like she wouldn't have any present for her boyfriend.

The best thing would probably be an IOU coupon. I could paint him one and then get him the book later, she thought, glad that she hadn't entirely forgotten about Kevin's birthday.

Kevin, feeling guilty about what he had just said, tried to change the subject quickly. "Say, Ricki, have you decided if you want to go to the dude ranch with me? I have to tell the magazine on Monday at the latest."

Ricki looked at him with sadness and also with incredulity.

"No, Kevin, up to now I've had other things on my mind."

"Well, then, think about it. It would be for next weekend, already."

66

"Next weekend?! I won't be able to go. Diablo needs to be walked, and I don't want to leave him alone now!" answered Ricki spontaneously.

"But Diablo can't be ridden anyway. A few days won't make any difference," said Kevin, obviously disappointed.

"If he has to stand in his stall all week, then those few days will be important! Anyway, I don't think I could enjoy the vacation if I knew that Diablo was standing around at home and couldn't even walk right due to my negligence. Can't you understand that?"

"Not exactly," admitted Kevin.

"Then think about Leonardo. How did you feel when your horse was in pain after being beaten during the training sessions with your father? Could you have taken a vacation on a dude ranch then?" Ricki wondered where Kevin's feelings were.

Kevin turned red in the face with anger and shouted at her.

"That was mean! Really mean! You know that was something completely different, don't you?"

"Why?" Ricki wanted to know. "Pain is pain, or isn't it?"

Kevin didn't answer anymore. One last time, he ran the brush through Sharazan's mane before he shut the stall door loudly.

"Don't be mad," begged Ricki. "I didn't mean to hurt your feelings!"

"But you did!" Kevin put his brush away and stomped off to the tack room.

"Could you two please stop it?" asked Lillian. "I think all of us are in a bad mood today. Maybe it's the humidity and the heat."

"How about going outside for a while? We could take pitchforks and clean up the paddock at last," suggested Cathy.

"Good idea," said Lillian and put Holli back into his stall.

Cathy grabbed two pitchforks, handed one to Lillian, then took up another. Together the two girls disappeared into the tack room, where Cathy gave Kevin one of the pitchforks without saying anything.

"Come with us!" Lillian ordered.

"Work duty on the paddock!" Cathy joined in and pushed Kevin out the door before he had a chance to refuse.

"Whatever," he growled and walked on in front of the girls.

"He didn't mean what he said," Cathy whispered to Ricki. "Try to understand him. After all, he thought he was giving you a nice surprise by inviting you along on his prize-winning vacation."

Ricki nodded. "You're probably right, but I thought anyone who had his own horse would understand why I couldn't go."

"He does," said Lillian. And that ended the conversation.

Chapter 5

The friends were pushing two wheelbarrows loaded to the brim with horse manure toward the paddock gate when Lillian glanced at the road and began to glow with pleasure.

"Hey, there's Josh!" she yelled. She dropped her manure fork, ducked under the paddock fence, and ran onto the road.

"Hey, lonesome rider, what are you doing here?" she called to him from a distance.

"Well, what do you think?" he answered back merrily as he stopped Cherish in front of Lillian. The young man bent down from the saddle and gave Lillian, who was standing on tiptoes to reach him, a hello kiss.

"This is my cousin, Melanie," he introduced his riding companion, who was staring over Lillian's head, looking bored. Melanie ignored the introduction—and Lillian—without a word of hello.

What a snob! was Lillian's first impression of the girl, but since she was a relative of Josh's, Lillian reached out her hand to be friendly.

"Hi, Melanie, it's nice that you came along. Do you like

it here? Has Josh taken you to Echo Lake yet? It's really lovely there at this time of year."

Josh's cousin ignored Lillian's hand and gave her a haughty look.

"Echo Lake? Is that what you call that mud hole in the middle of the woods, where the quacking of the ducks drowns all conversation? Yeah, we rode by there about two hours ago. The mosquitoes almost bit me to death, but this 'wonderful' horse here was unwilling to go any faster than necessary. I don't know why Josh chose this sleepy old nag for me!"

Lillian's boyfriend laughed.

"Orpheus is more than just okay. He's a mixture of Arab and Haflinger, but he's extremely gentle. He's a perfect horse for beginners!"

Melanie Stark blushed.

"What do I need with a beginner's horse? I have been riding for almost a year now," she said angrily.

"And still not steady in the saddle, as I realized during our one and only gallop!" Josh added.

In the meantime, Kevin and Cathy had joined the others.

Melanie, who had had an angry reply at the tip of her tongue, completely overlooked Cathy, but her facial expression changed immediately when she saw Kevin. She smiled her prettiest smile and, practically dripping with honey, said, "Colin! How lovely to see you again!"

"Hi, Melanie!" smiled Ricki's boyfriend, somewhat embarrassed by the overdone greeting.

"Who's Colin?" a confused Cathy whispered to Lillian.

"What are you doing with that wheelbarrow?" Melanie wanted to know.

"We just gathered up all the horse manure from the pad-

70

dock. Hi." Ricki had arrived a little after the others and answered Melanie's question before Kevin could reply.

"Hey, Ricki, this is Melanie. Are you finished with that chore?"

Ricki nodded. "Yeah, we just transported four wheelbarrows full up to the stable."

"Good job!" Josh looked over at the meadow. "Anyone mind if I check?" he asked grinning. He steered Cherish in the direction of the paddock gate.

"Wait," shouted Lillian, who already knew what Josh was planning to do. "Let's carry all the things out of the paddock first. We wouldn't want Cherish to step on a pitchfork!"

She ran back to the paddock with Ricki and then Cathy following her. Kevin was left alone with Melanie. He wasn't sure what to do, but he knew it wouldn't be polite to ignore a guest.

"Why do you have to clean up the paddock?" Melanie asked in a sugary-sweet voice. "Don't you have a stablehand?"

"Sure," explained Kevin, nicely, "but first of all, Jake is old, and second, a stablehand doesn't work in the paddock, and third, we help take care of our horses ourselves."

"Your horses? Oh, yeah, I remember. Josh mentioned something about there being two circus horses in the stable. One of them belongs to you, doesn't he?"

Kevin nodded. "That's right."

"Then this wonderful Chico, who opened the main door during the fire at the riding academy a few months ago belongs to you." Melanie looked at Kevin to see if she had impressed him with her knowledge, but he was laughing.

"You've managed to get everything completely mixed

up, Melanie. Chico is Lillian's donkey and the miracle horse at the riding academy was—rather is—Ricki's horse, Diablo."

"Oh, it must be because of the heat that I'm confusing things today." Slightly embarrassed, she lowered her eyes, although she continued to observe Kevin secretly. *He's real cute,* she thought. What had Josh told her about him? Ricki was his girlfriend! She glanced quickly toward the paddock.

What does he see in her? She's not very pretty...and those jeans and T-shirt are so grubby! she thought.

"Shouldn't we join the others? Let's see what Josh wants to do," Kevin offered.

Melanie felt a little awkward. "You know what, I'd rather stay here," she said. "I have the feeling that Lillian doesn't like me very much. She didn't even say hello to me," she lied and was delighted to see that Kevin stepped closer to Orpheus.

That's strange, he thought. *Lillian is usually nice to everyone.*

"Well whatever," he agreed, "we'll just watch from here."

Josh and Cherish put on a real Western show. He had his horse do fast spins on her hind legs and a sliding stop, making the girls hold their breath as Cherish came to a halt just in front of the paddock fence. Josh laughed, enjoying himself immensely. As he came to the end of the show, he knotted the reins around Cherish's neck and rode the horse by thigh pressure only.

Lillian's mouth hung open in awe. Ricki and Cathy were also totally impressed and applauded loudly. Cherish had

72

performed beautifully and uniquely. There was nothing she didn't do perfectly. Whether it was turns, slalom, or reverses, this horse didn't need to be helped with the reins. Just the slight, almost unnoticeable, pressure of Josh's thighs and change in position was enough to show the horse what was wanted from her. Even stopping and walking backward were performed on command.

For the finale, Josh had his horse gallop in a circle twice and then rear up on her hind legs in the center.

"Something like this is possible only on a completely clean meadow," the young man smiled as he rode out of the paddock.

"And on a wonderful horse, I'd say," answered Cathy.

"With a super rider," added Lillian proudly.

"Kevin, did you see that?" shouted Ricki, and turned around. "Kevin?"

Bewildered, she looked all around.

"Where did he go?"

"Melanie is gone too," realized Josh.

"Terrific! Just what I thought," said Ricki softly.

"They're probably in your stable. After what I told my cousin, I'm sure she made Kevin show her your horses."

"You can't make Kevin do what he doesn't want to do! If he does something, he does it voluntarily or he doesn't do it at all!" Ricki began walking toward the stable feeling slightly out of sorts.

"Colin knows what he's doing," said Cathy, joking.

"Who?"

"Kevin. Don't tell me you don't know your boyfriend's new name?"

Since Ricki continued to look at Cathy as though she belonged in an insane asylum, Lillian explained.

"Melanie baptized him with the new name a little while ago."

Even Josh just shook his head and looked sympathetic. "Melanie has a thing for unusual names—and a few other things as well. To be honest, I'll be glad when she goes back home at the end of next week. She just doesn't fit in here. She's a completely different kind of person than we are."

Ricki smiled at Josh gratefully. She felt the same way he did, but was a little uneasy that he said he would be relieved when she left.

"I don't like it when someone has to be in the limelight and has a big mouth, always putting down other people, always negative," he added, as the four headed for the stable.

"Hopefully, Kevin won't fall for that girl," Lillian said quietly to Cathy, as she noticed that Ricki's expression seemed to harden all of a sudden.

"Nonsense! Kevin and Ricki are a couple," replied Cathy.

"Exactly!"

* * *

"Well, did the meadow pass the expert's test?" Kevin asked, laughing, as Ricki entered the stable first.

"Hmm," she said and looked straight at Melanie, who had tied up Orpheus by his reins in the stable and was looking innocent.

"Why did the two of you disappear without saying anything?" Ricki wanted to know.

"Melanie was very anxious to meet our horses. She's thrilled with Sharazan," Kevin explained proudly.

"Yeah, that's right," confirmed Melanie. "At home I ride at an exclusive riding academy. They have beautiful and very well-trained animals, but Sharazan, he's really something special. You don't see a horse like him every day, do you, Shari?"

Melanie turned around and stepped closer to the stall in order to touch his forehead, but the animal suddenly laid back his ears and Melanie jumped away frightened.

"What's wrong with him?" she asked shakily.

Ricki smiled, but her eyes spoke volumes.

"Maybe he doesn't like to be called 'Shari.' His name is Diablo, by the way! Sharazan is two stalls up. Didn't Colin tell you that? And even if you can't remember names, you seem to understand something about horses. After all, you recognized that Diablo is a very special horse—just like every horse is *special*—something that is not necessarily true of your exclusive riding academy!"

Ricki was really on a roll, and Melanie looked helplessly at Kevin.

"Colin, please tell your girlfriend that she can't talk to me like that. It's…it's just incredibly rude!"

Kevin wasn't comfortable defending Melanie, but he felt compelled to do it. He didn't understand Ricki's behavior either.

"Hey, what's that supposed to mean?" he asked, confused. "Are you in a bad mood because of what happened earlier, or what?"

Ricki still smiled but her expression seemed frozen on her face.

"No, Kevin! But I'm sure that you will agree with me that one of the first things you learn when you frequent an exclusive riding school every day, is that you never tie up a horse by the reins! After all, it could break its jaw on the snaffle if it spooked!" Ricki pointed to Orpheus.

Melanie smiled back sweetly.

"This nag here supposedly can't be spooked by anything."

Now Ricki was really furious.

"First of all, this 'nag' is a wonderful horse, and second of all—and I'll say this slowly so you can write it down—HORSES ARE NEVER TIED UP BY THE REINS! Especially not in this stable! Do you have that yet?"

Melanie pretended to be helpless and started crying.

"Colin, is this girl in charge here?" she asked whining. The 14-year-old was really good at playing the victim.

"I'm sorry," answered Kevin. "This stable belongs to her parents."

"Good," sniffed Melanie. "Then I'm going to complain to her parents!"

"God, you are such an affected little creep," Ricki burst out. "Sorry, Josh, but I would have exploded if I hadn't said that."

Lillian's boyfriend nodded understandingly.

"It's okay," he said, and then Melanie attacked him.

"Excuse me? You think it's okay if someone insults me? This is unbelievable! You know what? You are the last….no…the *absolute* last—!"

Josh grabbed his cousin's hand. "Melanie, let's go! I'm ashamed of you in front of my friends," he said sternly. "But before we go, you have to apologize for your behavior."

"I won't budge an inch out of this stable, before *she* excuses herself!"

"You'll have to wait a long time for that!" screamed Ricki back at her.

"Melanie, untie your horse right now!" Josh's voice was getting louder.

"I'm never going to ride this old nag again! This isn't a horse, it's a joke!"

"That did it!" Ricki went dangerously close to Melanie. "Get out of here right now! Move it!"

"No!"

"Out!"

"Say you're sorry!"

"Never!"

Melanie stepped back as Ricki got even closer.

"Ricki, please, this isn't worth it!" Kevin tried to calm his girlfriend, but she just yelled at him.

"Kevin, don't interfere!"

"Now you've gone too far. After all, you really did insult her, didn't you?"

"Out!" screamed Ricki, completely beside herself. "Get out, or I guarantee I will throw you out!"

"Ricki! Stop shouting in here! Do you hear me? You're making the horses nervous!" Jake's voice thundered through the corridor. "Are you two completely crazy?"

As fast as he could, the old man ran over to Melanie and stared at her with eyes that bored into her.

"I don't know who you are, but after hearing all this, I would like you to leave this stable now! Normally, this is a quiet place and not for fighting!"

With a bright red face Melanie pressed past Jake without saying anything and hurried outside. When she went past Ricki, however, she hissed at her, without letting the others hear: "Just wait, you'll be sorry for this!" then she left on foot for the long walk home.

Although she walked quickly so that she would be off

77

the Sulai property, she couldn't help hearing Jake's voice once more.

"Which idiot tied up this horse by the reins?"

Lillian and Cathy stood pale and quiet in the corridor. They had never seen Ricki that angry, except for the time she had seen Diablo's former owner Frank Cooper mistreat him.

Kevin intended to follow Melanie on his bike. He couldn't leave her alone like this. Shaking his head in puzzlement, he walked past Ricki on his way out of the stable.

"Why did you get so upset?" he asked his girlfriend.

Ricki wanted to scream: *Because I don't want to lose you and because that stupid witch only rides because it's the* in *thing to do,* but she said nothing. She was too shocked herself at her overreaction.

On the other hand, Josh explained the whole incident to Jake objectively and precisely, and when the young man had finished, the old man could almost understand why Ricki had behaved the way she did.

"I think you'd better go," Jake said to the remaining three teens with a glance at Ricki, who was standing with Diablo unable to say another word.

Cathy and Lillian left silent, while Josh mounted Cherish and took Orpheus on a lead from Jake, who had brought him outside.

"Don't be too hard on Ricki," Josh begged Jake. "My cousin is no angel. Everywhere she goes, she starts a fight. I think she's only happy when she's making trouble. Please tell Ricki I'm sorry for Melanie's behavior. It was a mistake to bring her here."

He really left, thought Ricki. *He probably put her on the handlebars and rode her home! Oh, God, I've ruined our friendship because of that ridiculous cow—and my stupid jealousy,* she admitted to herself.

Diablo stretched his neck over the edge of the stall and rested his head on Ricki's shoulder to comfort her. He knew how his two-legged friend was feeling.

Ricki sniffed loudly.

"I'm sorry if I scared you and the others," she said to her horse, "but you have to understand, she insulted you wonderful creatures, and it looks like she has taken Kevin from me, too. Oh, I love him *sooo* much! Why didn't he stay here with us? Why did he have to ride his bike back after that idiot? Why?"

The next day Ricki stood nervously in the stable and brushed her shiny black horse. She felt guilty about losing her temper the previous day. This morning, before starting to work, Jake had put his arms around her and given her a hug to show her that he understood how she was feeling.

She was sure that Lillian, Cathy, and Josh wouldn't blame her. But how would Kevin act toward her today? Would he be mad or distant? Furious or sad? Indifferent or—?

Please not indifferent, thought Ricki. *There's nothing worse than just walking past each other without saying anything.*

Would Kevin even come to the stable today? After all, they had parted yesterday in complete disagreement.

"And why does today have to be his birthday?" Ricki groaned aloud. She had painted a beautiful picture of a horse last night for him. It was supposed to be Sharazan

79

standing on a huge ammonite at sundown. Underneath she had written: "IOU for a book about ammonites." Afterward, she had carefully rolled up the sketch paper and tied a pretty ribbon around it.

The picture turned out pretty well, if I do say so myself, she thought. She took it with her to the stable and hid it in the tack room.

I wish it were 3 p.m. already, but every time she looked at her watch, time just seemed to stand still.

Lillian and Cathy arrived about 2:30 p.m. They left their raucous laughter at the stable door and entered with serious faces, feeling awkward. They found it very uncomfortable to have experienced Ricki's outburst of temper yesterday. Kevin's girlfriend probably thought she had to excuse herself now to every single one of them.

"Hey, Ricki, you okay again?" asked Lillian cautiously, when she discovered her in Diablo's stall.

"Hello, you two. Yeah, I'm okay."

"Is Kevin already here?" Cathy walked over to Rashid as though nothing had happened. Lillian rolled her eyes. *You couldn't have asked a more stupid question right now,* she chastised Cathy in her mind.

"Do you see him?"

"No"

"So, why did you ask?" Ricki's insecurity was almost palpable.

She looked out of the window just about every other minute, but Kevin was nowhere to be seen.

"I can't stand it anymore! He's probably still mad because of yesterday. Maybe that bimbo got to him. If Kevin doesn't care then he can just stay away!"

80

"But Ricki, he wasn't going to be here for another half hour anyway. Don't forget, today's his birthday. He might be on the phone, or anything. Anyway, I'm sure he doesn't have a problem with what happened yesterday."

Ricki just swept Lillian's words aside.

"Normally he's here at the stable earlier than we said. You don't really believe that it has to do with his birthday?" She was planning to let them convince her otherwise.

"I'm going for a walk!" she decided impulsively and turned to leave.

Hopefully, she wouldn't run into Kevin. To be honest, she dreaded hearing that Kevin had fallen in love with that stuck-up beast.

"Should I come with you?" asked Cathy, but Ricki shook her head firmly.

"No! I think I'd rather be alone right now," she answered as she left the stable.

Cathy gave Lillian an all-knowing look.

"Serious love problems!" her lips formed soundlessly, and Lillian nodded. She had understood.

Just as Ricki was walking away from the stable, Cathy pointed over to the fields.

"Look, there he comes," she called.

At these words Ricki pulled herself together and mulled over whether it would be better to keep walking and avoid Kevin, but she decided to stay there and face him. Maybe everything would be okay again if she just wished him a happy birthday and gave him the IOU as though everything were normal.

Ricki went back into the stable as though nothing was wrong. She devoted herself completely to Diablo. She stroked him continuously while she told him in a soft voice where they would go when his leg was completely healed.

"And until then, we'll just go for walks, okay, my sweetie? While other people go to a dude ranch, we'll enjoy ourselves here, okay?"

Diablo looked at Ricki with gentle, understanding eyes. He loved his two-legged friend and enjoyed it when she talked to him so tenderly. Not to mention the delicious stroking she was always doing.

So what if he couldn't walk right now. Ricki was there and that was the most important thing.

"Hey, Kevin! Happy Birthday!" yelled Lillian and Cathy in unison, greeting him in front of the stable. Kevin laughed heartily.

"Even Carlotta didn't congratulate me so off-key," he joked as he parked his bike and carefully removed a large bag from the handlebars.

"My mom baked a cake for all of us," he said, and took out a large box from the bag. "Chocolate Mud Cake—I hope you like it!"

"Absolutely, great!" Cathy was enthusiastic.

"Ha! We like everything," agreed Lillian, and suddenly she felt hungry. She could never say no to cake!

"Where's Ricki?" Kevin asked as normally as possible.

"Here!" Ricki stood in the doorway a little unsure of herself. "Hello, Kevin, I wish you the best and I want to tell you that what happened yesterday, well, you know, I'm really sorry. Maybe I was just too upset after Diablo's accident—"

Kevin smiled. "It's okay. Melanie isn't mad at you anymore, either. I told her that you had had a bad day."

Ricki swallowed and had to control herself not to say anything mean.

"We have a present for you," Lillian told him and punched Cathy to remind her.

"Right!" confirmed her friend, giggling. "A present that was a lot of trouble for us," she added. Then she ran out to her bike and lifted a carefully wrapped package from her bike carrier.

Now Ricki was really curious. She had no idea what the two of them had thought up.

"Unwrap it!" Lillian could hardly wait to see the surprise on Kevin's face.

While Kevin slowly undid the knots in the ribbon tied around the box, driving the two girls almost crazy, Ricki ran over to the tack room to get her present.

She returned a moment later and stood next to her boyfriend, waiting while he slowly took off the lid of Cathy and Lillian's gift.

"Wow! That's terrific!" an excited Kevin shouted. Ricki looked over his shoulder and saw a large ammonite.

"Hey, thanks. This is really a great present!" He gave each of the two girls a big kiss on the cheek, and then he turned to the fossil and observed it intensely.

"Do you recognize it?" asked Cathy. "Lillian had to talk to Josh for hours until he finally agreed to give it up!"

"Well," Lillian said, with a side glance at Ricki, "I thought since Ricki's search at the quarry had been so unsuccessful…well, anyway, happy birthday—from Josh, too!"

"Thanks! Thank you so much! I'll phone him later!" Kevin was ecstatic.

"I have a little something for you, too," said Ricki softly and held out the rolled paper.

"Huh? What's this?" Kevin was really interested in finding out, but while he tried to undo the ribbon, he kept staring lovingly at the ammonite.

"Imagine, this morning Melanie came to my door and gave me something, too. You have three guesses. No idea? Well, I'll tell you. She brought me a fabulous book about prehistoric rocks. Really cool. I would never have thought that she would give me a gift, much less something that great." Kevin laughed with delight while Ricki went pale.

She gave him my idea! went through her head. *My idea! How weird! And anyway, why would she give him a present at all?*

In the meantime, Kevin had unrolled the paper.

"Oh," he said, now feeling a little embarrassed about what he had just said. "It's a really beautiful picture, Ricki. Thanks a lot!" He didn't know what to say. "Can I change the IOU to something else? I already have a book like that from Melanie." He chuckled. "She was just a little quicker than you were. I think that's really funny. What should we do?" he asked.

Ricki's eyes were filled with tears of rage.

"I don't think it's funny at all!" she answered. "I don't know what you're going to do, but I do know what I'm going to do!"

She reached out and grabbed the picture out of his hand and tore it in a thousand pieces.

"Since you already have everything you want, you don't need my present anymore. Why don't you go to Melanie and celebrate your birthday with her?" she said, calmly try-

84

ing to control her emotions. Then she turned and ran into her house.

"You idiot!" said Lillian. Then Cathy asked, "Did you have to say that?" Kevin just stared, baffled, after Ricki.

"What did I do wrong this time?" Kevin shrugged his shoulders.

"If you don't know, then I feel sorry for you," Lillian replied.

Chapter 6

Sharazan and Rashid were already waiting in the stable corridor, freshly groomed and wondering why they hadn't been saddled. Bored, first one and then the other scraped his hoof on the cement floor, while Diablo, Holli, and Chico looked over their stalls curiously. Something was different today.

Ricki hadn't come back, and the three remaining friends were sitting on hay bales eating the delicious chocolate cake.

"When is she ever going to get here?" asked Cathy impatiently. Lillian and Kevin found themselves going over to the stable door again and again to stare outside. They were waiting for Carlotta, who had promised to show them something of her former work as a horse trainer and equestrienne in the circus.

"If she doesn't get here soon, I'm going to saddle up and ride out," said Kevin, who had not said another word about Melanie since Ricki left.

"Don't be so nasty. Carlotta will be here any minute, I'm sure," said Lillian.

"Who's being nasty?"

"You!"

"Why? Because I want to go riding? Well, Ricki isn't here either. She's sitting in her room and sulking. What's the difference?" Kevin turned his back to Lillian.

"Look, it's your Sharazan, not Diablo, that was a circus horse. Anyway, I think that your leaving would be really rude toward Carlotta. After all, she did ask us if we wanted her to show us how she worked with the horses and we all said yes and agreed to a date. You were just as enthusiastic as we were, so don't sit around and complain!"

Lillian was upset.

"Or do you have other things on your mind in the meantime?" She looked at Kevin, waiting for an answer.

"What's that supposed to mean?"

Suddenly he got the message.

"You mean Melanie, don't you? What are you trying to say? She's a nice girl, that's all there is to it!"

"Well, no, thank you," the words slipped out of Cathy's mouth. "She's not my idea of a 'nice girl,' but maybe that's because I'm a nice girl myself!"

"That does it! Why are you all against her?" Kevin's voice got harsher but Lillian said candidly: "That nice girl wants to steal Ricki's boyfriend, and the idiot doesn't even realize it! Do you know Colin? He's—"

"Oh, shut up! You've read too many romance novels!" Kevin got up abruptly, turned around, and bumped right into Jake, who was standing behind him.

"Sorry," mumbled Kevin. "I need some fresh air!"

The old man stared after him.

"It looks like Kevin is sitting between two chairs. Where's Ricki? In the house? Those two should get together as soon as possible and talk!" Jake started to leave, but when he got to the door, he turned around.

87

"Carlotta's here! What's she doing here at this time of day? She always comes much later."

"She's going to show us some of her circus routines."

"What? Do you want to play circus?"

"Sort of," Cathy laughed.

Jake shook his head in disdain.

"Instead of being glad that none of the horses show circus manners when they're ridden, you're promoting the stuff again. Well, I don't approve of those drills. An animal is much more beautiful if it's allowed to move freely, not forced to do stupid tricks. When I think of the monkeys dressed up and made to ride on shy ponies… No, that's a kind of cruelty to animals, too!" Jake's disapproval showed on his face.

"We're not planning to put sweaters on our horses and we're not going to force them to do anything. After all, Sharazan and Rashid performed in the circus ring for several years. The two of them can probably do it in their sleep."

"Stupid tricks! I'd never let my horse do things like that."

There was no reasoning with Jake today.

He must have missed his nap today; he's in a terrible mood, assumed Cathy to herself.

"I'm glad that Diablo doesn't have to do that stuff," he said, and stamped out of the stable with a furrowed brow.

"Circus crap!" he mumbled loud enough for the others to hear.

When Carlotta finally drove up the gravel drive and got out of her car in a happy mood, Lillian and Cathy were already running toward her.

88

"Hello everyone! How are you? Horses groomed and otherwise everything okay?" she asked in her friendly way.

"Well, that depends how you look at it. Jake is totally against circus 'crap' as he called it, and is totally against Diablo learning any circus moves. Ricki is in her room alone, trying to think clearly. She had a fight yesterday with Josh's cousin Melanie and today with Kevin. He's acting as though he's the victim, because I think he's fallen for that girl. Ricki is jealous, but other than that, we're fine. And you?"

Carlotta laughed heartily, dispersing any tension in the air.

"Thanks for asking. I'm great. I'm raring to go today. According to your report, I have the perfect conditions for my performance. Kevin, come here!" Carlotta's voice didn't allow any contradiction, so Kevin, who had been standing in the distance, came back to the girls.

"I suggest that we begin right away," said Carlotta. "Kevin and Cathy, you two bring the horses out onto the paddock, and Lillian, get the long training whip. If you don't mind, I'm going to drive this thing down to the meadow. I'll have to stand long enough! Kevin, I think I'll choose you to assist me."

Carlotta glanced around waiting for their approval. However, although Lillian and Cathy nodded to her, Kevin stubbornly looked away.

"Is there some other problem?" asked Carlotta, looking right at Kevin.

For a moment, Kevin was silent, but then he burst out:

"I'm not in the mood for circus performing anymore! I don't feel like it at all. Ricki is pouting somewhere; she doesn't seem to be interested anyway. The two of them—"

89

he nodded in the direction of Cathy and Lillian, "are talking nonsense, and I'm in a bad mood. No thanks! It's all stupid stuff! Jake's right. Everything about it is crap!"

He turned around abruptly, intending to leave quickly, but Carlotta's thundering voice made him stay.

"Kevin! Who do you think you—? Stand still when I'm talking to you! Do you think I have nothing better to do than stand around here and teach you how to perform in a circus? I swear I would be glad to do it if you were really interested, but now I have better things to do with my time!"

She lifted one crutch and pointed it at Kevin. "My dear boy, I don't know what's going on here, but I can see that you're not your usual self. If you have a problem, then I'll give you some good advice, if you want it. But you shouldn't keep it all bottled up inside—it's important to communicate. That means talking about it. That's what having a girlfriend is for. Ricki will be glad to listen."

Kevin, annoyed, rolled his eyes and had a get-real look on his face.

"I'm supposed to talk with her?!" he grumbled. "The whole mess is her fault. Anyway, she just threw me out of her room!"

Carlotta was about to respond, but Lillian beat her to it.

"I think you must be out of your mind! Just because today is your birthday, you don't have the right to say stuff like that. Are you crazy? First, you let yourself be sucked in by that pretentious Melanie—Colin this, Colin that— and then you get ticked off when Ricki's mad that you're flirting with Josh's cousin. Maybe you could think a little before you say these things!"

"Women! Of course, you all stick together! You know

what? Just leave me alone with all that talk! It's really starting to get on my nerves!" He turned quickly and ran off.

"You've done a great job, Mr. Thomas! Really fabulous! Thanks a lot!" Cathy furiously yelled after him.

Carlotta put her arms around the girls' shoulders, both of whom were trembling with anger.

"It's not that big a deal girls," she said and smiled. "He'll calm down in a while, but you have to understand that it's impossible to work effectively under these circumstances. Your nervousness would make the horses nervous, and then you can forget about a performance. Anyway, Sharazan is Kevin's horse, after all, and we can't work with him without Kevin's approval."

Lillian looked at Carlotta with disappointment. "I'm so sorry, Carlotta. You took the time especially for us. Who knows what's gotten into Kevin. He's changed completely ever since he met Melanie Stark."

"Yes," agreed Cathy. "It's as though Kevin has fallen for her. He doesn't admit it, but his eyes give him away. Ricki noticed it right from the beginning, and yesterday, here at the stable, she was furious, especially when Melanie started trashing her own horse, Orpheus. You know Ricki, that kind of thing really gets to her!"

Carlotta nodded, then she stepped back and got into her car. Before she drove off, she put her head out of the window.

"I know our Ricki is very sensitive. But Ricki and Kevin are both stubborn, and if they don't talk with each other, the situation will only get worse. If you want to do something for the two of them, try to get them to sit down and talk, so that it can be cleared up. After all, they do like each other, and it shouldn't be that hard to talk about what happened."

Of course it was much more difficult than Carlotta had thought.

Ricki and Kevin continued to avoid each other the following week. When Kevin appeared at the stable to take care of Sharazan, Ricki stayed in the house until he either went riding or went back home.

Lillian and Cathy found the situation totally ridiculous and never knew whether they should stay with Ricki or go riding with Kevin. Usually, Kevin left before the two girls could decide what to do. Other times, while Ricki occupied herself intensely with Diablo, Lillian and Cathy went riding with Kevin.

The three girls usually spent the evening together at the stable and tried to be as cheery and carefree as they used to be. They avoided the topic of Melanie and Kevin, but Ricki's heart was heavy with sadness all the time.

The one good thing was that Diablo was obviously getting better. He could already take a few cautious steps, and Ricki decided on Wednesday that she would take him outside in the fresh air for a few minutes.

With every yard the two of them went, Diablo seemed to walk more sure-footed and with less pain. After about 15 minutes, Ricki returned to the stable with a beaming face and announced that she would be able to walk her horse for half an hour the next day.

"That's great!" responded Lillian. "I'll go with you. It'll be good for me, too, to take a walk and get a little exercise instead of letting Holli carry me around all the time," she added with a chuckle.

Cathy made a sour face. "Unfortunately, I don't have any time tomorrow. Mom's driving to my aunt's house right after lunch for a visit. She's my godmother, and Mom said it might be nice if I went with her, especially since it's her birthday. I'd much rather go for a walk with you two than sit at a table and have coffee and cake, but I promised."

Sometime that evening they sat in the stable and talked about Kevin, who had been in to see Sharazan for only a short time that day.

"Friday, really early, he's leaving for that riding weekend," Cathy offered somewhat cautiously.

"It's Stony Ridge Ranch, isn't it?" asked Lillian, and Cathy nodded.

Ricki looked a little upset.

"Do you have any idea who's going with him?" she wanted to know and looked at her friends, suspecting the worst.

Lillian and Cathy looked at each other with desperation. What could they say not to hurt her any more than necessary?

"Well, ah… I'm not sure, really. I think that…" stammered Cathy, and looked pleadingly at Lillian, who was older and usually could think of the right words.

"Ahem," Lillian cleared her throat. "It looks like…but don't get the wrong idea. Josh told me that—"

"Melanie!" Ricki felt her whole being collapse inside her. "It's not enough that ever since she showed up nothing is right between us anymore, that she gives him presents and spoils my surprise for him! No, now she's talked him into taking her along on his prize-winning weekend." The tears welled up in her eyes. "I would never have thought that Kevin could let himself be so easily manipulated. Doesn't he see that that *bimbo* just wants to break us up?"

Ricki got up from the bale of hay and ran to Diablo's stall.

Lillian followed her friend and gently put her arm around her waist. "Ricki, I don't know how to tell you this," Lillian began again, "but Josh said it was Kevin who suggested it to Melanie. She called her mother right away, and it looks like she's allowed to go. It seems Melanie lives not far from the ranch."

"That's how it is, then," Ricki said softly. God, it hurt so much to lose Kevin. She had known that would happen from the first time Kevin had told her about Melanie.

"He said today that he won't be coming to the stable to-morrow because he has to pack and take care of a few things before he leaves on Friday," Cathy told the others.

Ricki let the words go right by her, and her friends couldn't tell if she had heard them or not. The three girls stood silently by the stalls; the only sound was the breathing of their horses.

"I feel a little sick," Ricki said a few minutes later. "If it's okay with you, I think I'm going to lie down."

Lillian and Cathy nodded, full of sympathy. They would probably feel the same way if they were in her shoes.

After Ricki had disappeared into the house, the girls decided to leave for home as well, but as they walked to their bikes, Lillian said, "I don't understand Kevin. Why is he doing this to her? Do you think he really has fallen for Melanie?"

Cathy shrugged her shoulders uncertainly.

"I have no idea, but I don't like the whole thing either. Ricki is so upset. I feel so sorry for her."

"Me, too. Oh well, maybe things will work out. But right now Kevin seems to be blind to everything. Otherwise he would see how calculating Melanie is by throwing herself at him. She probably doesn't care anything about him. She's just doing that to hurt Ricki. I think Josh was right when he said that she causes trouble wherever she goes."

Lillian got on her bike and waved good-bye to her friend.

"Well, so long. Maybe Ricki will be able to get her mind on other things tomorrow when we go for a walk with Diablo. Have fun at your aunt's house," she said grinning.

"Oh, I almost forgot!" groaned Cathy. "I'll be thinking of you both while I listen to my aunt complain about my tomboyish ways. See you Friday then. Take care." And the two friends pedaled off in opposite directions.

Ricki was completely exhausted when she woke up early the next morning. She tossed and turned all night and the little sleep she did get was made restless by confusing dreams:

She had recognized Kevin and Melanie, walking hand in hand through the countryside. Diablo, who Ricki had tied up somewhere, whinnied happily to the two of them as he recognized Kevin. When they got close to the black horse, Melanie went up to him and untied his rope, and then slapped him on the croup, sending him galloping off in fear. She watched him with a sneering grin on her face, as he stumbled and fell down.

"That's giving Ricki what she deserves," she said haughtily, and linking her arm in his, she walked away with Kevin, who seemed totally indifferent. Then they got into the train that would take them to Stony Ridge Ranch.

What a dream! thought Ricki as she got dressed, still feeling a little queasy in her stomach. *She would really do it, I'm sure of it. I hope I never have to see her again!*

Taking in deep breaths of fresh air, she arrived at the stable a few minutes later, where Diablo whinnied a good morning greeting to her.

"I'm so glad I have you," said Ricki, as she drew the horse's head to her lovingly. "This afternoon we're going to take a nice walk. We'll see how far you can go without pain. What do you think? Should we walk toward Anderson's meadow? It's at least a little shady there."

Diablo looked at Ricki knowingly. He loved it when Ricki talked with him like this. In answer, he snorted in her hair, making her laugh in spite of her somber mood.

"Okay, that's a date. We're walking to Anderson's meadow this afternoon! But first, my darling, I'm going to make you beautiful, okay?"

Ricki opened the stall door, gave her horse a treat, and lead him out to the corridor. Then she got her grooming basket from the tack room. She glanced at the damaged saddle and sighed deeply. She had a feeling it wasn't fixable.

"Darn!" she said aloud, but then her gaze fell on Diablo and she put all thoughts of the damaged saddle away. She was overjoyed that her horse was on the road to recovery.

"A saddle can be replaced, my sweet. You couldn't have been," she whispered softly to him, and began to carefully brush his coat.

Chapter 7

Ricki and Lillian stood with Diablo in the stable corridor, having gotten everything ready for their walk.

They hadn't heard anything more from Cathy or Kevin, of course, and, at the moment, that didn't seem important. Both girls were looking forward to the walk on this beautiful day.

Ricki carefully scraped out Diablo's hooves before she put on his snaffle. Then she turned to Lillian and cheerfully said, "As far as I'm concerned, we can go. The two of us are ready."

"Super! Let's go."

Lillian left the stable first and waited outside for Ricki, who slowly and carefully lead Diablo through the doorway.

"I think it's best if we walk on the soft edges of the meadow. His leg won't be jolted as much as if we walked on the paved road or the uneven field roads," said Ricki, and Lillian nodded in agreement.

"I think so too. That'll be best. Do you know which way you want to go?"

"I thought we could go to Tom Anderson's meadow," said Ricki.

Lillian was totally pleased with that suggestion.

"Great! It's so beautiful there. All those fruit trees and the peace and quiet...you feel like you're on top of the world, on the condition, of course that Tom Anderson isn't emptying manure there!" Lillian wrinkled her nose at the thought and then joined in Ricki's laughter.

"They're actually going for a walk with that black nag! I would never have thought of that. Don't they have anything better to do?" Melanie muttered to herself.

She had borrowed her cousin's bike and was out riding around when she discovered Ricki and Lillian just by chance, as they walked slowly along the edge of the meadow with Diablo.

Melanie had actually intended to go to town to buy a few little necessities for her weekend at Stony Ridge Ranch: a new blusher and eye shadow and some sparkly nail polish. After all, you might meet some interesting boys on the ranch and, if you did, then appearance was everything if you wanted to win them over.

But for some reason, she hadn't turned toward town. Instead she was on the back road on the way to the Sulais' farm. Did she want to check and see if Kevin said good-bye to Ricki after all? Melanie didn't know herself, exactly; she had just ridden off and something instinctual took over.

To be honest, Melanie didn't really feel like going away with Kevin, but anything seemed better than staying here in the sticks with nothing to do, especially since Josh had refused to take her anywhere with him again. Besides, she saw it as a chance of getting even with Ricki for insulting her.

Melanie smiled nastily at the thought of revenge.

"You are such an idiot, Ricki Sulai, and your Kevin isn't much better either. He's always bragging about you. But after this weekend, you two won't have anything more to say to one another. I'll take care of that. No one insults Melanie Stark and gets away with it!" she said to herself quietly.

An idea came to Melanie for a fraction of a second, but she rejected it immediately. However, the longer she watched the two girls with the horse, the more a plan took shape in her mind.

"I'll show you, Ricki Sulai! You won't be able to forget me!" She hissed quietly, and began to pedal more quickly. She had a good idea where they would be heading. She rode far enough away so that neither Ricki nor Lillian could see her, and finally managed to get ahead of them but still keep them in sight.

Ricki, in the meantime, had decided to leave the meadow and take the narrow path that was the shortcut home. She didn't want to overdo it with Diablo. The path was bordered on one side by a ditch overgrown with bushes on the edge of a wood and on the other side by a field where cows grazed, fenced in by low barbed wire.

"It's pretty narrow here," said Lillian, who was walking behind Ricki and Diablo.

"Yeah, but it's direct," said her friend, who carefully watched Diablo to make sure he didn't misstep.

"I think, when we're home, that will be enough for him today," said Ricki, who had noticed that her horse had been walking more slowly the last five minutes than he had at the beginning of their walk.

Melanie crouched in the underbrush about 30 yards from Diablo. Her bike was a little farther away, leaning against a tree.

Just like a spider in a web, she waited for the little group to walk by her. Feeling a rush of excitement, she kept trying to see through the bushes but was careful to not let herself be seen.

Soon, she thought, *you're going to get a real surprise, you stupid cow.*

Diablo was just about opposite the girl crouched in the brush. Melanie heard Lillian and Ricki laughing together, and the sound of their jovial camaraderie filled Melanie with such jealousy that any scruples she might have had about acting on her plan vanished completely.

Keeping very still, she silently counted to 10.

Now! she thought, and she herself was frightened by the sound that suddenly was heard echoing through the woods loudly and shrilly like a siren.

Ricki's and Lillian's hearts almost stopped. They were petrified.

"What's that?!" shouted Lillian and observed with horror what was happening before her eyes.

Diablo reared straight up in the air in panic, and the whites of his eyes were clearly visible.

Ricki was so terrified that the reins slid out of her hands when Diablo reared up.

"DIABLO! NOOOOO!"

She stumbled and fell, while Diablo, frightened to death, tried to escape the shrill sound by galloping away, but his reins got caught in the brush.

The sound seemed to be everywhere.

Diablo tried once more to bolt. This time his injured

100

joint bent away again. The horse attempted to get a sure hold on his three healthy legs, to maintain his balance, but in vain. Unsteady, stepping to the side, his injured leg collapsed and Diablo fell to the ground.

An inhuman scream tore through the air. Ricki's heart stood still. She tried to get up and run to her horse, but her legs refused to hold her.

Once again, Diablo let out a savage scream that caused the girls' blood to freeze in their veins. Ricki suddenly realized what had happened.

"Oh God, no! The barbed wire!" She managed to get up and ran to her horse, who was lying on the ground wildly waving his hooves about. He was still trying to stand, but every time he moved, the barbed wire, which had been pulled off the posts, wrapped itself more tightly around his legs and his neck. Diablo was almost crazy with panic.

"DIABLO! Diablo, be calm my darling, be calm. Stay still, otherwise you're going to hang yourself! My God, Lily, do something, I, I— " Ricki felt as if she were going to be sick.

Paralyzed by their helplessness, the two girls stood about a yard from the thrashing horse and could only watch while he became increasingly caught up in the barbed wire.

"DIABLO!" screamed Ricki again, and Lillian, who was chalk white, tried to keep her friend from going closer to the horse.

"Stay here, Ricki, do you hear me? Stay here, for heaven's sake," she shouted at her.

"Diablo is killing himself! I can't just stay here and watch. We have to help him!" screamed Ricki and tried to get out of Lillian's grasp, but her girlfriend seemed to have incredible strength today.

She shook Ricki violently, trying to get her to come to her senses.

"You're going to stay here, Ricki Sulai! Do you understand me? Look how Diablo is kicking—you can't go near him!"

"Let me go! Right now!" she screamed, struggling to break free. "Let me go…let me…*gooo*," Ricki's voice was drowned in her desperate sobs. Suddenly, weakened by fear and panic, she collapsed.

Lillian got down on her knees beside Ricki, wrapped her arms around her, and hugged her head to her chest. Gently, she rocked her sobbing friend back and forth and stroked the hair out of her eyes while Ricki starred vacantly at Diablo. The horse's movements had become increasingly limited before they stopped all together. And with a soft whinny, the horse lay still on the ground.

Suddenly it was dead quiet around them. At some point, the siren had stopped, and Lillian realized that not even the birds had begun to chirp again. All life seemed to be frozen after what had just happened.

Ricki, racked with sobs, turned her eyes away from her beloved horse and to her companion.

"Is … is he … dead?" she asked Lillian in a small, toneless voice just before her entire body began to tremble like a leaf in the wind.

Lillian's tears ran silently down her cheeks in streams.

"Say something, Lily," begged Ricki desperately. "Please…say…th-that…he…is…s-still…alive," she stammered through her sobs.

Lillian took a deep breath and looked heavenward for help.

"Ricki…I…I don't know," she answered softly and

102

hugged her friend even closer, as though by holding her tightly she could make everything go away. At the same time, Lillian knew that she was holding onto Ricki because *she* was afraid to get up and look more closely at Diablo.

Lillian's "I don't know" had broken something inside of Ricki. Her fingers, which had been clamped to Lillian's arm, had lost all of her strength. Hiding her eyes in her hands, she wept uncontrollably.

But after a minute or so, she willed herself to stop crying, took several deep breaths, and moved apart from Lillian. With a face wet with tears, she nodded weakly to her friend and even attempted a little courageous smile.

"I'm … going to look… I have to know," she whispered without expression, and then awkwardly got up on her shaking legs. She saw Lillian's tearful eyes and turned very slowly in Diablo's direction.

When she saw Diablo laying on the ground completely still, it took a great deal of strength to keep going, to put one foot in front of the other and get close to him. She was terrified with fear that she would look into his lifeless eyes.

Suddenly Lillian was beside her.

"I'm going with you!" she said firmly, and Ricki reached for her hand, full of gratitude, while she her gaze remained unwaveringly on her horse.

She tried to call her black horse softly by his name, but her throat was constricted and she couldn't speak. She took several more deep breaths and, moving faster now, within seconds she was kneeling beside Diablo's head.

"Oh, God…why?" she whispered softly while she carefully touched her horse's forehead with trembling hands. Slowly she let her eyes wander along his body. She wanted to scream and cry at the same time, she was so miser-able.

"I th-think…he's…d-dead," she stammered, and felt as if she were going to faint.

A barbed-wire loop in which Diablo had become entan-gled was tight around his neck, and the barbed wire had torn his coat and bored itself deep into his flesh. Blood flowed from countless wounds and had gathered in a large pool under the head of the lifeless horse. Desperate, Ricki tried to loosen the wire, but no matter what she did, it was impossible.

"That darn siren, or whatever it was," whispered Lillian and swallowed her tears.

In rage and misery, Ricki lifted her head back and cried out her pain and suffering, while her hands rested in a red sea on Diablo's neck.

Melanie had observed the whole thing. At first she really enjoyed it when Ricki fell and it looked as though Diablo would run away. But as the animal began to stumble and became entangled in the barbed wire, all the color went out of her face. Diablo's horrible screams made her tremble. She managed to turn off the loud pocket siren, which she carried with her at all times for her safety.

"What have I done?" she whispered from her hiding place, where she remained paralyzed with fear.

Now that Ricki was yelling so loudly, Melanie forced her-self to her feet and ran as fast as possible toward her bike.

I've got to get away from here before someone sees me, she thought, while she raced through the woods. If she wasn't so scared, she would have stopped to throw up be-hind a tree, she was so sick in her stomach.

Ricki bent over Diablo and hid her face in his long mane. She felt exhausted and empty. Lillian stood helpless across from her.

"I'm going to run to the nearest farm to get help," she said to Ricki, but her friend didn't respond.

"Is that okay with you?" she asked again and finally saw Ricki give a slight nod of her head.

"Good. Can I really leave you alone here?" she asked uncertainly.

"Yeah, thanks," breathed Ricki without looking up.

Lillian turned around and began to think feverishly. Which way should she go? To the Anderson farm or maybe to Bob Holland, who lived nearby in a small hunting lodge on the edge of the forest?

In any case, first straight through the woods, she thought. *When I'm through it, I'll decide what to do then.* Determined, Lillian took off.

After about 150 yards, she saw a bike rider on the path in front of her pedaling as fast as he could.

Where did he come from? she wondered, baffled, as she continued to run so she wouldn't lose any time.

Ricki sat beside her lifeless horse for a long time. Desperate and with a heavy heart, she was now incapable of any more tears. It was awful to sit there and do nothing. She had to do something. Softly, she spoke to her beloved horse.

"Why? Diablo? Tell me why? You can't leave me alone. It's not fair, do you hear me? That's just not fair!"

With heavy limbs she crawled around the animal and decided to try to free him somehow from the horrible wire.

"Even if you aren't aware of it anymore, my darling, I

can't stand to look at it any longer." Without thinking, she took off her T-shirt and wrapped her hand in it. Then, working mechanically, as if she were on autopilot, she very carefully began to untangle first one leg and then another from the jumble of wire. Now that Diablo had stopped moving, she was able to do it pretty quickly.

At last she had loosened the wire enough so that she could also loosen the loop of wire around his neck and slip it off.

"At least you are finally free of that," she said softly. But as she removed the snaffle from her horse, she was overcome with tears. She removed the bloody T-shirt from her hand and pressed it onto the wounds on Diablo's neck that were still bleeding.

"Diablo, you know that I loved you very much, don't you? I…I wa…I want to thank you for all the won-wonderful hours you have…given me. I never th-thought for a moment that I could lose you…and if…then certainly not like this."

Ricki sobbed and sobbed, overcome by her sadness and tears.

"What should I do now, all alone? Why did you go? Why?"

Mechanically, she kept wiping off the blood.

"You wonderful horse. I will never—do you hear me? Never ever forget you. You were my best friend, the best I could have ever imagined. Thank you for your love, for everything you gave me in the short time we had together. Good-bye, my friend. I will never, never forget—I swear it. And always—Are you listening? I will always carry you in my heart. You were the greatest—no, the *absolute* greatest joy in my life."

Ricki broke down completely. The shock she was in up to now seemed to dissolve suddenly, and she fell over Diablo's body, and in her misery began to beat upon it with her fists.

"I DON'T WANT YOU TO GO! DO YOU HEAR ME? I JUST CAN'T STAND IT! COME BACK! DIABLO. PLEASE! YOU KNOW I NEED YOU!" she shouted into the silence of the woods.

Lillian felt as if her heart would burst as she pressed the bell at the Andersons' house with shaking fingers. First just for a second, and then she held the button down continuously.

"Why don't they open the door?' she wondered out loud. "Surely they aren't all out in the fields?"

"Hello," shouted Lillian. "Is anybody home? Hel-loooo!"

She hammered on the door and rang the bell nonstop.

Just then Tom Anderson came out of the stable. "Well, good heavens, what's going on? Who's making such a fuss?" Furious, he hurried as fast as he could toward the "troublemaker," waving the pitchfork in the air threateningly.

"Oh, God, it's you, Lillian." he realized as he got closer. "My old eyes and my ears aren't what they used to be anymore," he said somewhat embarrassed, and then leaned his pitchfork against the house.

"Please, Mr. Anderson. You have to help us…and I have to use the phone, it's really important."

"What happened? Is something wrong with your father or mother?" interrupted the farmer, very concerned now. After all, he knew how quickly an accident could happen on a farm.

"No, no, Mr. Anderson. My parents are fine. It's only that—" and then Lillian poured out the whole horrible experience. "I have to phone Dr. Hofer, but I think Diablo is dead. At least, he wasn't moving anymore."

Tom Anderson listened intensely.

"What an awful thing to have happened," he said then, and gestured for Lillian to come into the house immediately.

"555–7576," he said as he handed her the receiver.

"Excuse me?" Lillian didn't understand.

"555–7576—the phone number of the vet. I know it by heart by now," said the farmer.

"Thank you." Lillian dialed the number with trembling fingers and swung her foot back and forth nervously.

"Hello? Dr. Hofer? Thank God, you're there! It's Lillian Bates! You have to come right away, something terrible has happened. No, not at our farm. It's about Diablo. What? No…yes. He got entangled in a barbed-wire fence and is lying on the path between… Oh, God, how can I explain it?"

Without saying anything, Tom Anderson took the receiver out of Lillian's hand and described the place where Diablo lay. He knew where it was because of a few specific things Lillian had mentioned before. After two or three more questions from the vet, he hung up the phone.

"There, help is on the way. Now, Lillian, try to calm down a little. We'll get my car and drive there. The vet will be there soon."

"I'd like to phone Ricki's parents, too," Lillian said quickly, but Tom Anderson shook his head. "You can do that afterward. At the moment, the only one who can help is the vet. If I know Mrs. Sulai and her timidness about horses, she'll just make her daughter more anxious than she is already. Come on now, let's get a move on, otherwise Doc Hofer will be there before us."

Lillian agreed and followed the farmer to his car. Within minutes, they were on their way to the woods.

Ricki jumped in alarm. What was that she heard? Was she starting to hallucinate? If she didn't know better, she would have sworn she heard Diablo snorting.

There! There it is again!

Now I'm going crazy, she thought and glanced over at the horse's head, nervously. Had she been mistaken or had his eyes moved a little?

Ricki's whole body began to tremble yet her senses became acutely alert.

"Diablo?" She spoke softly to the horse she had assumed was dead. She thought she would faint when she saw that one of his ears had turned toward her a bit.

"Oh, God, he's alive!" Suddenly dizzy, Ricki was barely able to prevent herself from blacking out, but a few deep breaths helped. With her heart beating like a jackhammer, she crept closer to her beloved horse's head and held it in her lap. Tears of relief and happiness started to flow down her cheeks and onto the animal.

Diablo looked at Ricki with his huge, endlessly loving, trusting eyes. Ricki was there, nothing else would happen now. Totally trusting that his friend would take care of him, the horse closed his tired eyelids.

Ricki spoke soothingly to him. "Don't go back to sleep, my darling…are you listening? Don't go to sleep. You have to stay awake. I am so glad that I have you again. Come, I'll tell you a story, Diablo…Diablo? Hey! Wake up! Yes, that's right. Look at me, then I'll know that you're alive. God, thank you for giving him to me a second time. Thank you, thank you, thank you!"

Tom Anderson and Lillian arrived almost at the same time as Dr. Hofer at the beginning of the meadow path, where they had to leave their cars and continue on foot.

The vet jammed his bag under his arm and ran behind Lillian, who had gone on ahead. Tom Anderson followed after them, but more slowly.

"Is it far?" asked the vet as he walked, and Lillian shook her head.

"No! Up there. Where the bushes are especially high, that's where it happened," she answered. She would have liked to stop for a few seconds to catch her breath. First of all, she was completely exhausted, and second, she dreaded seeing Ricki sitting next to her dead horse. She would carry that picture in her mind forever.

Ricki saw Dr. Hofer and Lillian running toward her and uttered an audible sigh of relief. Completely oblivious to the fact that she was sitting there with no shirt on, in just her bra and jeans, she carefully put Diablo's head onto the ground and stood up awkwardly. Her foot had gone to sleep.

She began to wave.

"He's alive! Diablo is alive!" she called loudly.

The surprising yet welcome news caused Lillian to stop in her tracks, which almost made Dr. Hofer run smack into her.

"No!?" she yelled back, and a big smile began to spread across her face.

"Yes!"

"Get out of the way," panted the vet, out of breath, and shoved Lillian aside. "Sorry, but if the animal is still alive then there's work for me to do!"

The bloody T-shirt was still lying on the horse's neck as Dr. Hofer knelt down in front of Diablo.

"I am so glad to see you," said Ricki, stepping out of the way so the doctor could get to her horse. "Diablo must have fainted. He woke up just a few minutes ago."

Dr. Hofer took a quick look around in order to get an idea of how the accident happened. When he saw the enormous piece of bloody barbed wire and the extent of injury to the horse, he realized how much Ricki had done to free the horse from the wire.

Quickly he assessed the horse's condition. He saw that the many cuts all over Diablo's body were very deep, and that the neck area was especially badly injured.

"This all has to be cleaned and stitched up," said Dr. Hofer quietly, more to himself than to the others standing nearby. "Thankfully, Lillian mentioned the barbed wire. It causes a great deal of damage. As a country vet, I've seen a lot of that. The stuff should be forbidden! Thank goodness, I have everything I need with me."

"Don't we have to get him to an animal clinic?" asked Ricki, who, in the meantime, had put on Tom Anderson's old jeans jacket and was now kneeling beside Diablo.

"We'll see. I'll have to examine him further. Ricki, give me the stethoscope—the thing with the long tubes in my bag—yes, exactly, and I need the little flashlight, too."

Carefully, the vet listened to the horse's heartbeat and examined his pupil reflex. Diablo lay still, as though he were anesthetized. Only his ears moved back and forth a little.

"His heart is all right and so are his reflexes," he said

111

softly. "The many little cuts are the smallest problem, but the injuries on his neck are worrying me a bit. The wire cut in pretty deep. It's bled a lot, I can see. At the moment we can only hope that the airway or the esophagus hasn't been injured as well."

Ricki turned pale.

"What happens if they are?" she asked, frightened.

"Then we'll have to operate—and quickly. But don't get upset in advance. I'm going to examine him closely. Bring me my bag, please, and put it down here, beside me. Thanks. And if you can't stand the sight of blood, turn around. I can't treat anyone who faints!"

Lillian and Tom Anderson turned aside immediately. Ricki, on the other hand, who, today, had gotten used to blood and the way Diablo looked, remained standing beside the vet.

Dr. Hofer smiled briefly. "Is my assistant nurse ready? Can we begin?"

Ricki swallowed hard before she nodded.

"Okay!"

"Well, here goes!"

The vet put on a pair of gloves and gave Ricki a second pair.

"Put them on, and then open the silver box. There are sterile gauze pads inside. As soon as I say so, hand me a few of them."

Ricki did as she was told.

First Dr. Hofer took care of the injury on the neck. In order to see how deep it was, he couldn't avoid pulling the wound apart, although it had finally stopped bleeding. But right away it started to bleed again, and Diablo shuddered with pain.

112

"Gauze pad!" ordered Dr. Hofer, and Ricki obeyed blindly. She could feel her horse's pain.

"Well, as far as I can tell, there are no internal injuries. Luckily, Diablo has very thick muscles on his neck. That means that as soon as we disinfect the wounds, we can sew them up. There are several layers of skin on his neck that need to be patched, but if you help me, Ricki, nothing can go wrong. You're really a great assistant."

Ricki inhaled deeply and tried to smile. Her attention was riveted on Diablo as she awaited the vet's next order.

"I should have phoned the Sulais," said Lillian, after a while. "I'm sure they are worried. Especially since Ricki's disappearance with Diablo only a few days ago."

"You can call them on my cell phone," said Dr. Hofer, who had been listening. "It's in the car. Please tell them that we'll be busy here for at least another hour, if not longer, before I'm finished with Diablo!"

"I will," shouted Lillian and ran toward the car.

Chapter 8

Over the next few hours, Ricki got to know firsthand the various surgical instruments Dr. Hofer used to repair Diablo's wounds. There was a scalpel, which he used to clean up many rough edges. These were a special scissors to cut away pieces of skin that were too damaged to save. There were wound clamps, with which he could hold pieces of skin together so they wouldn't slip out of his fingers, and other instruments to hold the wound open so he could treat the inner skin layers. In addition, there were tweezers, one flat and one serrated; huge round needles that could be attached to one of the tweezers and used to sew up the cuts; and a tiny scissors to cut the thread. Dr. Hofer had two different kinds of thread in a closed, sterile spool box, and Ricki was amazed when the vet explained to her that this thread was called catgut or cat silk.

The vet had spread out a large piece of rubber on the ground beside Diablo and then placed a large sheet of sterile cotton on top. While he explained everything to Ricki, he opened a large silver-metal box, in which his instruments were stored, and began to lay them out onto the cotton. He put the box with the gauze pads next to them, then reached in with a clamp, pulled out several of them, and laid them on the cloth as well. Lastly, he took out a disinfectant spray and a container of powder.

Once again, he reviewed his preparations and put on fresh gloves. He looked at Ricki, who was feeling a bit queasy after seeing all the instruments.

"Are you okay?" the vet asked and smiled encouragingly at her.

Ricki nodded. "Aye, aye, sir," she responded and knelt down in front of the cloth.

Dr. Hofer worked tirelessly and with total focus.

First he gave Diablo a tranquilizer to make sure that the horse would not get to his feet while he was stitching him up. He also gave him an injection to stabilize his circulation and give him a little strength before he started to work on the horrible neck wound. Then he gave the horse a local anesthetic so the pain would be minimal.

"Well, let's begin," he said to his pale assistant. "First I need the clamp to hold the cut open," he ordered. After that, he just gave her short instructions.

"Gauze. Scalpel. Come here and hold the clamp. That's right. Pull it back a little so I can get to the muscle tissue—stop, not so far. Yes, just like that. Hold it still, right there. You're doing very well, Ricki!"

Dr. Hofer cleaned and disinfected the wounds before he snipped away the ragged edges and began, layer by layer, to close them up.

Ricki was sick to her stomach but she never would have admitted it. Although she had to look away at first, after half an hour she was able to look directly at Dr. Hofer's hands. How skillfully he managed to close the ragged cuts so that afterward all you saw was a narrow row of stitches.

It was the first time Ricki had been present when the vet worked liked this, and she was rather proud of herself for helping him after the worst cut had been taken care of. At least, she had helped a little.

Dr. Hofer worked systematically from the top down, and it went relatively quickly because most of the wounds were not as deep or as large as the neck wounds.

When he reached the pastern area, Ricki held her breath again until the vet said that the tendons that lay under the skin in this area had not been damaged.

After about an hour and a half, during which neither Dr. Hofer nor Ricki had looked up from Diablo, the vet snipped the last thread of the last wound and threw the tweezers with the needle onto the now blood-red cloth where the used gauze pads were piled up.

One last time he sprayed disinfectant over the stitches and checked to see that he had not missed any cuts.

"There," said Dr. Hofer, "that was the first side." Carefully he checked Diablo's circulation again, as well as the effect of the tranquilizer.

"I think I'll have to give him a little more," he said, and then he prepared the injection.

After he was sure that Diablo would remain in this dazed condition, Dr. Hofer waved Lillian and Tom Anderson over.

"You'll have to help us turn Diablo," he said to them, and he got them and himself into position beside Ricki. Together, the four of them managed to roll the horse over onto his other side.

"Here we go again," he said, and began to work on Diablo's other side, assisted by Ricki, who worked tirelessly as well as she was able.

116

She didn't know how much time had elapsed when Dr. Hofer was finally finished.

"Done!" he said, then he stretched out his stiff, aching back. Ricki, too, was exhausted. She had crouched during the entire procedure and now her legs were numb. Slowly she began to move her body, but before she got up, she bent over Diablo's head.

"My darling, it's over now. It might hurt a little in the next few days, but the pain will go away eventually. The main thing is that you will be completely healed." Lovingly she gave him a gentle kiss on his velvety nostrils.

The tranquilizer seemed to be slowly wearing off, and the horse's legs began to twitch slightly.

Ricki got up, stood next to Dr. Hofer, and took off her bloody gloves.

"Girl, you were wonderful!" praised the vet, putting his arm around her shoulder. "If you ever want to be an assistant vet, I would hire you in an instant—and that's a promise!"

"Thanks," replied Ricki with shiny eyes. "You weren't so bad yourself."

Dr. Hofer grinned.

"Well, you do what you can."

"I still have two questions," said Ricki, with her eyes on Diablo.

"And what are they?"

"First, I want to know why Diablo lay there so lifelessly. Did he really faint or something?"

"Hmm," said Dr. Hofer. "I think he was in shock. A shock can stop all body reactions temporarily. Why did your horse jump into the barbed wire in the first place?"

"A siren suddenly went off here, and he bolted."

"A what? There are no sirens here." Dr. Hofer looked at Ricki somewhat skeptically.

"I know that it sounds crazy, but that's what happened. Suddenly there was this shrill noise in the woods, and then, as unexpectedly as it came, it was over, but by then Diablo got entangled in the barbed wire," explained Ricki.

For a moment there was silence, until Ricki remembered that she had another question.

"How am I going to get Diablo home?"

Dr. Hofer began to put his instruments away.

"The best thing would be to organize a horse trailer and drive it as close as possible. It's too bad the path is so narrow here. Diablo is going to have to walk a little way before we can load him inside."

"Can he walk at all in this condition?" asked Ricki.

"Wait half an hour. When he comes to he will try to stand up. I'll give him another shot for his circulation. I'm sure he'll manage to walk that short distance, even if he's a little wobbly."

Now Ricki was relieved.

"We need a trailer," she shouted and turned around to Lillian, who, she thought, was right behind her.

She was totally amazed to see Jake and Brigitte standing about three yards away. Neither Ricki nor Dr. Hofer had noticed that the two adults had arrived. Their complete concentration was on Diablo, and Ricki's mother and Jake had stayed in the background so that they would not disturb the vet while he was working.

"Mom!" called Ricki, and ran over to hug her. "I'm so glad you're here," she said, and then corrected herself, "both of you!"

Brigitte and Jake were both chalk white and Ricki could see the worry for his horse in Jake's eyes, which were fixed on Diablo lying on the ground.

Gently Ricki stepped back from her mother and stood in front of the old stable master.

"Jake," she said gently. "He's going to be all right. And this time it really wasn't my fault. If only the darn siren hadn't gone off!"

"Why is he still lying there? Why doesn't he get up?" Jake didn't seem to be listening to her.

"He's still dazed from the tranquilizer."

With heavy steps, the old man slowly started walking toward "his" Diablo. In these last few hours, he seemed to have aged by years. As he approached the black horse, he relived all the moments he had shared with the animal. He would have never gotten over it if Diablo had died.

In the meantime, Lillian, who was standing next to Ricki, grabbed her and twirled her around exuberantly.

"Hey, you! I don't know what to say."

"Then don't say anything."

The two girls smiled at each other. The tension of the day was slowly beginning to fade away.

"We need a trailer," said Ricki again. "Do you think your father would take Diablo home one more time?"

Lillian nodded energetically. "Of course! What kind of question is that!" Brigitte reacted immediately.

"Come on, Lillian," said Brigitte, "Let's drive to your house. I hope your father is home."

"Where else would he be?" Lillian responded with a grin. "Our cows would complain bitterly if they didn't get something to eat about this time."

"Where's Mr. Anderson?" Ricki wanted to know.

119

"He had to go back to his farm," Lillian explained, then ran after Brigitte, who was already going to her car.

Ricki hurried back to Diablo, who was already trying to stand up.

Jake held his hands clamped together as if in prayer, while he observed Diablo.

Ricki stepped up to her black horse, and Dr. Hofer went on the other side.

"Okay, my boy, try again, I know you're going to make it!" she encouraged the animal. "You have to get up, then you've won. C'mon. C'mon." Lovingly she bent down and stroked his forehead. She looked deeply into his wonderful eyes and seemed to be having a silent dialogue with him.

You're strong enough to get up, she willed her thoughts to him. *Do it. I can't help you, unfortunately, you know that but if you want to go back to your stall, you have to get up. Do you understand? C'mon! Stand up, boy!*

Diablo let himself fall back down on his side, but less than two minutes later, he tried again. He stretched out his forelegs and then shoved his hind legs under his belly and pushed himself up with his last ounce of strength.

"That's super! You're terrific!" Ricki hugged his neck carefully. She was deeply moved by his courage. Jake, too, was very emotional.

As Diablo stood on wobbly legs, Dr. Hofer grabbed his stethoscope and listened to Diablo's heart.

"Everything's okay," he announced. "Now all we have to do is get him home."

"Lillian will be back soon, I'm sure," said Ricki, and she put the snaffle in her horse's mouth. She held the reins tightly, and stroked the horse continuously, encouraging

120

him to move. For one moment, she closed her eyes. She would never forget this day as long as she lived.

After about 20 minutes, Ricki heard Dave Bates' car and the noise the trailer made on the uneven path.

"They're coming," she shouted to Jake and Dr. Hofer, who were standing together talking about the accident while Ricki was happily occupied with her Diablo.

"Well, let's get this fellow loaded into the trailer," answered Dr. Hofer, and together the three of them got the horse slowly back down the path. Lillian's father had parked his trailer at the end of the path and had already lowered the loading ramp.

Without hesitating, Diablo allowed himself to be lead inside the horse trailer. He knew he was finally going home.

Just like the last time, Ricki stayed with her horse. She would feel completely relieved only when he was finally standing in his own stall at home.

Once again, Carlotta's words had proven true, she thought suddenly. *Usually something happens much quicker than you imagine.*

* * *

It was 7:45 a.m. when Kevin arrived on Track 3 at the train station, armed with a small travel bag and a backpack for his riding boots. His mother had driven him to the station, and, with a heavy heart, had already said good-bye to her oh-so-adult son and driven home.

Kevin looked at his watch nervously. The train would arrive in 10 minutes, then he and Melanie would take the two-hour trip to Stony Ridge Ranch, where they would be able to have a good time for three whole days.

121

"What's taking her so long?" Kevin wondered. He kept looking back and forth to see if he could find Melanie among the passengers who were beginning to fill the platform.

She arrived at the track at the last minute, just after the announcement that the train was arriving.

"I overslept," she defended herself. "I'm sorry, Colin. By the way, good morning."

"Morning," said Kevin, grinning, glad that Melanie had arrived in time. It wouldn't have been any fun to travel alone.

Then a voice on the loudspeaker announced, "The train is arriving on Track 3. Please be careful boarding." The passengers began to find their places on the platform according to where they would be sitting on the train.

"We have reserved seats in Section B," said Kevin, and picked up his backpack.

Melanie made a face. *As though I had never traveled by train,* she thought. She wished she hadn't said she would go; she wished she were at Josh's house. Bored, she walked behind Kevin, who was enthusiastically looking forward to the weekend.

After the passengers had boarded and the seats were filled and the train had started moving, Melanie looked at her traveling companion.

"Did you visit your horse yesterday to say good-bye?" she asked, not really interested in whether he did or didn't, but wanting to find out if he heard about what happened to Ricki's horse. Nonetheless her heart was beating rapidly.

"No," laughed Kevin. "I wanted to spare him and me the sadness of parting. You were downtown yesterday. Was it fun? Did you get everything you wanted to buy?" he asked her.

122

"Yeah," Melanie answered curtly and turned her head to look out of the window.

He still has no idea what happened, she thought, and suddenly she felt very uncomfortable with herself.

What had happened yesterday with Diablo, just because she had wanted to scare Ricki, had really upset her.

What will happen if they find out that the accident was my fault? she asked herself over and over. She had observed Josh the entire evening and tried to decide if she should tell her cousin what she had done and ask for his advice, but she hadn't felt brave enough. She had remained silent and then excused herself and gone back to her room, telling the others that she felt sick. Well, actually, she didn't have to pretend, seeing Diablo lying on the ground had really upset her stomach.

"Want a piece of gum?" asked Kevin, holding out the package.

Melanie shook her head. "No thanks," she said curtly.

"Is something wrong? You're so quiet today," Kevin observed, but Melanie just kept staring out the window.

"I'm just tired," she claimed, and returned to her silence.

Kevin shrugged his shoulders and relaxed in his seat. While he enjoyed the scenery, he thought about Ricki and the past week, during which they hadn't spoken to each other.

Unobserved, he glanced at Melanie and tried to figure out what was going on with himself. Was he in love with her like Lillian said? And what *about* Melanie? Was it possible she just wanted to steal him from Ricki in order to humiliate her?

Kevin thought about it for a long while, but he couldn't answer any of his own questions just yet.

He closed his eyes with a sigh and tried to imagine how

the weekend would go. How he would have loved to have Ricki there! To be honest, he already missed her, and the same was true of Sharazan. He almost wished he could get off the train at the next station and go back, but he couldn't do that to Melanie.

After all, she was so excited when I invited her, and so looking forward to it, Kevin thought.

Since he couldn't talk with his companion at the moment, Kevin settled in and soon the monotonous sound of the train on the rails put him to sleep.

After about an hour, Kevin woke up from his nap with a start.

"God, what's happening? Is something burning?" he shouted and jumped up from his seat. As he got up he realized that the other passengers in the car were also confused, and some were actually frightened as they crowded into the corridor.

A shrill ear-splitting siren had abruptly destroyed the peacefulness of the ride and continued wailing, filling the airwaves with a piercing, shrieking noise.

"Oh, man," yelled Melanie desperately. "I can't shut the thing off! It went on by accident. Nothing has happened. It's an ultra-loud pocket siren that I always carry with me so I could scare away a mugger in an emergency. Kevin, help me! The switch to turn it off is stuck!"

Kevin's heart was still beating in panic mode as he took the little apparatus, which was about the size of a deck of cards, and tried, in vain, to shut it off.

"Shut that thing off! It's unbearable! When children travel on their own something always goes wrong!"

"Children?! I'm 14!" Melanie protested, but the furious shouts of their fellow passengers drowned out her words.

Kevin felt as if he were going deaf. In his panic, he took the alarm, threw it on the floor, and stomped on it.

After the third try, only a tinny clicking noise could be heard, and after the fourth try, it was finally silent.

"Thank God! It was about time!" An elderly man angrily looked over at the kids. "If I had had another heart attack, it would have been your fault."

Since Melanie didn't even try to respond, Kevin turned to the man and said as nicely as possible: "We're really sorry. We didn't do it on purpose. Please, excuse us."

"Hmm," grumbled the man. "With all that darn high-tech nonsense nowadays, anything can happen. Thank heavens, it's broken now. If you hadn't stomped on it, I would have!"

Kevin was relieved when everyone had settled back into their seats and calmed down.

"Here," he said, handing the device to Melanie. "How could that happen?"

"I've no idea. It just went off. I probably bumped it when I tried to get a piece of chocolate out of my bag."

"Well, maybe you should offer everyone here some chocolate as a peace offering for the scare they all had," laughed Kevin. Melanie just rolled her eyes.

"Anything else?" she asked, and then remained silent.

That's her real character, thought Kevin, more than a little disappointed. *She can never say she's sorry for anything. She probably wouldn't have cared if the old guy had keeled over from fright—she's so cold-hearted. Ricki would have reacted completely differently.*

Yeah, Ricki, Kevin sighed, and then he opened his backpack and fished out a bag of fruit candy. He went from seat to seat with it.

"I want to say I'm sorry for the scare we just had…that my girl…that a friend of mine caused. Can I offer you a piece of candy to make it up to you?" he said to each of the passengers. Most of them smiled at him and accepted his apology.

When he returned to his seat, Melanie looked at him as though he were from another planet.

"Do I get one, too?" she asked him with raised eyebrows.

"Of course. I'm not Melanie Stark, who sits on her own hoard," replied Kevin and held the almost empty bag open for her.

"Thanks, I've changed my mind!" Insulted, Melanie hid behind her book.

"You'll have to replace my siren," she said without looking at Kevin.

Leave me alone, thought Kevin, and regretted deeply that he had invited her to come.

Almost automatically, he glanced at his watch. 9:07 a.m.

Thank heavens, we'll be there soon, thought Kevin, and hoped that there would be a lot of nice people on the ranch so he wouldn't have to deal with Melanie very often.

* * *

Dr. Hofer was at the Sulais' stable early the next morning to examine his patient.

"Well, how's my patchwork quilt?" he asked Diablo affectionately, while Ricki led her black horse out into the stable corridor.

"Isn't that a little mean?" asked Ricki grinning.

"Haven't you ever heard that people make fun of others'

126

misfortunes? But you're right, I shouldn't make fun of animals. How is our super boy?"

"I think it was harder on me than him," said Ricki.

"Where did you get that idea?" the vet asked while he examined the stitches he had made the day before.

"Well, last night Diablo lay down as usual and this morning he got up as soon as I came in. He greeted me exuberantly and ate all of his carrots. That's a good sign, don't you think so, Dr. Hofer?"

The vet laughed.

"And what about you?" he wanted to know.

Ricki groaned like a Hollywood diva.

"I dreamt of clamps and scalpels all night. It was pretty scary, especially since I tried to cut up a pork chop."

"Well, that isn't a very uplifting dream, but aside from that, I want to tell you that you did a great job assisting me. Not every horse owner could have done that. My compliments, Ricki, you can really be proud of yourself!"

Ricki turned red with embarrassment.

"Of course, after all, it was about Diablo. I'm so glad he's going to be okay. Can I take him back to his stall?"

Dr. Hofer nodded and then rummaged through his bag.

"I'll leave you some salve and powder. Check the stitches a few times a day and put the salve on the largest ones in the morning and evening. If anything starts to seep, put powder on it. If it's not better the next day, let me know and I'll come. Otherwise, you'll see me again in five days. Is everything clear?"

Ricki took the salve and powder and nodded. Sheepishly she looked at the vet.

"I don't think I've thanked you yet for all your help," she said softly.

"Your praise was enough, Ricki." Dr. Hofer smiled. "Okay, take it easy and take care of our patient. Don't let him get out and burst the stitches before they've healed."

"That would be awful! No, no, I'll never let him out of my sight again," promised Ricki seriously.

"That's all right, then. So, see you in a few days," said the vet and ran quickly back to his car, where his cell phone was ringing. Two minutes later, Dr. Hofer drove off with his tires squealing.

Ricki, who had watched him leave from the doorway, ran back to Diablo, who was looking longingly out of the window.

"No, my boy For the next few days the paddock is out of bounds for you, I'm afraid. When you're better, we can talk about it, okay?"

Peacefully, she looked at her horse and still couldn't believe that he was standing there in front of her. The terrible experience was still so fresh in her mind.

"You know what, sweetie? I'm going to get a book and sit down with you. I want to spend every remaining second of summer vacation with you," she whispered to Diablo. Then she left the stable to go to her room and find something to read.

* * *

"And when you've unpacked your things, come down to the dining room, please. We'll meet there and eat a late breakfast. After that I'll show you the horses. You're probably anxious to see them, aren't you?" Carmen Sanchez beamed at Melanie and Kevin, as though she had just adopted two little orphans.

128

"Thank you, Mrs. Sanchez. I can't wait to see what Dixie is like," answered Kevin politely, but without much enthusiasm. The ranch owner noticed it right away.

"Kevin isn't very happy at the moment," she said later to her husband, Alfonso. "And Melanie...I don't know... there's something funny about her."

"Oh, you with your psychology! If you had your way, we wouldn't have any 'normal' guests here on the ranch," said Alfonso, affectionately.

"That's true, in a way. The people who come here are looking for peace, relaxation, and some distance from the problems and worries of their everyday life," Carmen explained.

"And some just want to ride and be with horses—or they've won a prize," her husband added. "I'm going to the stables now!"

Kevin had put his bag in the closet of the cozy room. He didn't feel like unpacking just yet, so he went over to the window and looked out at the gorgeous mountainous landscape with lush, wide meadows and deep, green woods. In front of the ranch house were fenced in paddocks and horses frolicking on the meadows.

It's really beautiful here, he thought. While he watched two colts beneath his window chase each other across the paddock and make unbelievable jumps with their stiff little legs, he began to look forward to finally meeting Dixie. Nevertheless, he missed Sharazan more than he thought he would.

Kevin sighed, turned, and left his room to see if Melanie, who was in the next room, was ready yet.

Softly he knocked on the door.

"Are you ready yet? Can we go down?" he asked.

"I'm going to take a shower first," answered Melanie.

"Shower? Why do you want to take a shower when we're going to go to the stable in a few minutes?" Kevin just shook his head, perplexed.

"I don't feel like going to the stable right now, and I really don't feel like riding the stupid horses!" Melanie shouted.

"Then why did you come?" asked Kevin, puzzled.

"Oh, just leave me alone!" snarled Melanie behind the closed door. Kevin had no other choice but to go down to the dining room alone, and he felt really awkward.

Well this is starting out really well, he thought. *The only other thing that could go wrong is that Dixie goes lame, and I can't ride. If that happens I'm going home right away!*

Chapter 9

Ricky spent the morning reading in the stable. Actually, the book lay unopened beside her because she couldn't stop thinking about the events of the day before and all she had experienced, as well as about Kevin. She wondered if it was nice at the dude ranch and if he was having a good time with Melanie.

She had spent way too much time thinking about the two of them and was very glad to see Lillian and Cathy, who came by after lunch, bringing their good moods with them.

"Man, I can't leave you two alone for even one day without your getting into trouble!" joked Cathy before she went over to Diablo's stall to see how he was doing.

"Lillian told me everything. Man, oh man, I am *sooo* glad that he's alive!"

"Me, too. Believe me!" Ricki nodded in agreement, then turned to Lillian.

"What are you planning on doing today? Are you going riding?"

"Hmm, we wanted to but... Hey, couldn't you saddle Sharazan and come with us? He needs to have some exercise, too."

"Never!" Ricki shook her head firmly. "First of all, Kevin and I are not speaking. I don't want to make it worse than it already is. Second, I won't ride anybody else's horse without permission. Just imagine if something happened to Sharazan like what happened yesterday. Kevin would kill me! Remember what Carlotta said!"

"You're right," admitted Lillian, and stole a look at Cathy. Her friend knew exactly what she was thinking. The unspoken question was: *Should I tell her?* And the silent answer was: *I have no idea!*

"Why are you two eyeing each other so strangely? Did I say something wrong?" Ricki looked back and forth at the two girls and frowned. "You two know something. Spit it out! I hate this kind of secrecy."

Lillian sighed. "Okay. Let's sit down before you fall down," she said warily, motioning to the bales of hay in the corridor.

"What you're about to tell me can't be worse than what happened to us yesterday," said Ricki as she sat down.

"Well, okay, here goes. I called Stony Ridge Ranch today about noon," confessed Lillian.

"What? Why did you do that? Where did you get the telephone number?"

Lillian looked a little guilty.

"Kevin gave me the number so I could call him if there was a problem with Sharazan."

"And? Is there a problem with Sharazan?"

"Oh, Ricki, don't make it so hard for me. Of course, there's nothing wrong with Sharazan! But there's something wrong with Diablo…and…and I thought that Kevin should know everything. You two are more than just friends, after all!"

132

"Friends?!" Ricki snorted contemptuously. "Is it friendship when you can't talk with each other anymore? Anyway, you should have asked me first if I wanted Kevin to find out everything." Ricki was mad that Lillian had gone behind her back.

"Okay, you're probably right, I should have asked you first," admitted Lillian. "But when I tell you what I found out, you'll be glad I called Kevin. The mystery about what caused Diablo's accident seems to be solved."

Ricki jumped to her feet and stood facing Lillian with her hands on her hips.

"And just what does Kevin have to do with it?" she asked.

"Nothing, of course, but guess what happened in the train on the way to the ranch?"

"Come on, tell me!"

"Melanie had a pocket alarm with her. You know, a thing to—"

"I know what that is! Keep going," impatient, Ricki interrupted her friend.

"The thing went off, and the piercing siren scared the people in the train half to death."

"So what?"

"Ricki, don't you get it? The horrible sound that scared Diablo so much?"

"You mean…?" Ricki turned pale.

"I'm not sure, of course, but it could have been Melanie."

"I don't believe that! She's awful, but she wouldn't do something like that! No, I can't believe that of her." Ricki walked over to Diablo, shaking her head.

Lillian slowly followed her.

133

"What I haven't told you yet is that when I ran off to get help yesterday, I saw someone riding away on a bike very quickly."

Ricki remained quiet. Was it possible that Melanie was capable of such a thing? Could she have really risked costing Diablo his life just to have her revenge on Ricki?

"God, if that's true, then she's really sick," said Ricki, red-hot anger surging through her. "And she almost killed my horse!"

Lillian put her hand on her girlfriend's shoulder to calm her down.

"Kevin was shocked when I told him what happened, and he said he would find out if Melanie had caused the accident."

"Kevin isn't objective," Ricki said, but then she nodded. "But maybe now he'll get to know the other side of Melanie, if she really did it. I hope for her sake that she didn't have anything to do with it, otherwise…otherwise…"

Kevin turned pale as he listened to Lillian's report on the phone. He felt terrible that he wasn't home to support Ricki.

What in the world had he been thinking when he invited Melanie along on this weekend?

"Melanie!" he growled through his teeth. "How could I have been so wrong about her? I must have been blind! Blind, deaf, and stupid all at once!"

"Kevin? Are you ready?" Carmen Sanchez knocked on his door, then opened it slightly and stuck her head in. "Lunch!" she called happily.

Kevin kept starring at the phone, then he turned around slowly and announced, "I'm going home, Mrs. Sanchez— today!"

134

Carmen Sanchez pushed the door wide open and looked at him questioningly.

"Why? Don't you like it here?"

"No…I mean, yes, it's beautiful here, but— "

"Do you want to talk about it?" she asked full of concern, but Kevin shook his head.

"No, I…I have to clear up something," he said, and suddenly he ran past the woman and, without knocking, ran right into Melanie's room.

Melanie squealed in surprise, but when she saw who it was she started to yell at Kevin angrily.

"Haven't you ever heard of knocking before entering a lady's room?" she shouted at him. Kevin's icy-cold stare made her stop talking immediately.

"Lady?!" said Kevin as he approached her frighteningly slowly. "I don't see a lady here. All I see is a nasty, selfish little child who smears makeup on her face with a trowel to cover up her mean character."

Melanie turned white.

"Colin, I—," she began in a sweet voice.

"My name is Kevin! K-E-V-I-N! Where were you yesterday afternoon?"

"What's going on? Is this some kind of interrogation?"

"I want to know where you were!"

Melanie put a bored look on her face.

"In town, you know that. Now get out of my room."

Kevin stared at her long and hard with a look of fury and Melanie felt a growing panic.

He knows! she realized with horror. *It's over! What can I do?*

Kevin still said nothing.

"Colin…Kevin, I—"

"Why?" exploded Kevin. "Why in the world did you do it? Diablo is such a wonderful horse! How could you do such a thing?"

"Ricki...I hate her!" said Melanie without any emotion.

"You wanted to hurt Ricki? Well, you managed to do that, all right! You are so low! Diablo is—"

Melanie collapsed in a flood of tears.

"I didn't want him to die. You have to believe me. I just wanted... It's just that Ricki has everything I always wanted and never had. Friends, a horse, her own stable—and I hate her! I hate her, hate her, hate her!"

Sobbing, she threw herself onto the bed. Kevin had the impression that probably for the first time in her life this emotional outburst was not fake.

I should tell her that Diablo is alive, he thought, but decided to remain silent. *She should feel bad a little while longer. She should know what it's like, so she understands how much Ricki suffered!*

"I don't want to have anything to do with you again, you snob! And leave Ricki alone from now on! I'll never let anyone hurt her again! I'm ashamed to even know you!"

With that, Kevin turned and stormed out of the room, his heart beating wildly. He went next door and began to pack his bags. He just wanted to go home.

Carmen Sanchez was still standing in the hallway and had heard everything. She looked at the sobbing girl and shook her head. *The things these young girls are capable of,* she thought to herself. *Jealousy can turn you mean and ruin everything!*

"I want your parents' telephone number," Carmen said in a stern voice.

Melanie got off the bed, wiping her tears away with the

136

back of her hand. On wobbly legs she went to the dresser and began to search though her handbag. She handed Carmen her father's business card.

"You can start to pack your things," Mrs. Sanchez said in a harsh voice. "People who are cruel to animals and are jealous and hateful are not welcome here. When you're finished, wait in your room until someone comes to pick you up! Understand?"

It was about 5 p.m. when the train rolled into the local station.

I'm finally home again, Kevin thought as he put his bag on his shoulder and adjusted his backpack. *Why in the world did I ever leave? I'm such an idiot!* As he stood on the platform, he closed his eyes for a moment and took several deep breaths.

The man at the ticket counter, who had handed him the reserved tickets just that morning, was perplexed that the young man was again walking through the railway station.

"Hi, back already?" he called after him, but Kevin was too preoccupied with his thoughts to hear him.

He headed toward the phone booth next to the station entrance.

"Mom?" he asked seconds later into the receiver. "Don't be upset. No, nothing happened. Can you pick me up? I'm back home. What? No, no. I'll tell you all about it later. Okay, see you soon. Bye."

Kevin hung up and stepped outside onto the plaza. Slowly he walked over to a bench and sat down feeling emotionally drained.

In his mind he was already with Ricki at the stable. He

137

wondered how Diablo was today. How would Ricki react when he stood in front of her? Would she forgive him for his idiotic behavior?

Kevin lifted his head and stared into the bright blue, cloudless sky. *Life could be so wonderful if people didn't cause problems for others,* he thought, and all of a sudden he felt very grown up.

Melanie's mother picked her up at Stony Ridge Ranch. They sat silently in the car, neither one saying anything to the other.

Carmen Sanchez had told Sandra Stark about the conversation she had overheard, and Melanie's mother was very ashamed of her daughter. Deep down she knew that what she heard was the truth.

She clenched the steering wheel as she drove and thought about her daughter, while Melanie sat in the passenger seat as far away from her as possible, trying to disappear into the soft leather.

If only Mom would speak to me, she thought desperately. *This silent treatment is making me crazy.*

After driving for a while, Sandra Stark suddenly turned off the road and parked at a rest stop. She kept starring straight ahead out the window, still holding onto the steering wheel.

"Okay, Melanie," she said then. "I want to hear the whole story from you, and I want the truth—with all the details—do you understand me? So talk, I'm listening."

Melanie thought for a moment about telling her mother a made-up story, one like those that had often gotten her out of difficult situations before.

Sandra Stark turned to face her daughter. "I said, the

truth!" she repeated emphatically. "Not some story that you just made up. Lying is over, once and for all!"

Melanie's body shuddered involuntarily. *Mom always knew!* she realized, ashamed. Tears came to her eyes. Then she took a deep breath and faced her destiny.

"Everything started when Josh gave me that stupid horse, Orpheus, to ride," she began with a soft voice. And for the first time in her life, Melanie managed to tell the truth. The picture of the lifeless Diablo caught up in the barbed wire as he lay on the ground had so burned itself into her conscience that she couldn't think of anything else. Melanie wished she could make this picture vanish, and knew that could happen only if she dealt honestly with the situation.

For half an hour Sandra Stark listened to her daughter's version of the events with disappointment. She was forced to admit that Melanie was one of the most arrogant, selfish, egotistical people she had ever known.

What did I do wrong in bringing her up that caused her to be like that? she kept asking herself.

After Melanie poured out the whole story, her mother needed a few minutes to deal with all she had just heard. Silently she looked into Melanie's face before she started the engine and drove back out onto the highway without saying a word.

Expecting some kind of reaction from her mother, Melanie was uncomfortable by the silence. So after a few minutes back on the road she said, very cautiously, "I think you took the wrong exit just now…" But Sandra Stark just kept driving.

"You are going to apologize," she said with no warning. "That's the least you can do. You are going to stand in front of this girl, Ricki, and look her straight in the eyes. And your apology, my daughter, will not be the usual offhand kind I know so well from you. You better hope that she accepts your apology. Otherwise, the picture of that horse will be in your mind for the rest of your life."

"Mom, no! I can't apologize to her," Melanie began to whine dramatically.

"You're going to! That's all there is to it! I'm driving right to the stable, and I'll be listening to everything you say to that girl. Do you understand me? This time you are not going to get out of dealing with the consequences of your behavior," she said in a tone that was unusually harsh for her.

Melanie felt dizzy. If she could have, she would have fled.

Mom is mean…very mean! thought Melanie and continued to sulk.

***

Ricki had tied up Diablo in the corridor of the stable and was smearing the salve onto his wounds. Jake stood beside her watching everything she did.

"You should put a little more on that one, up there, and you forgot one back there."

Ricki rolled her eyes a little.

"I'm not done yet, Jake," she said while she tried to follow his instructions exactly. "Don't worry, I'll check everything all over again before I take him back to his stall," she promised. Jake, however, watched her with mistrustful eyes.

Lillian and Cathy were out riding. Sharazan stretched

140

his head over the side of his stall and began to nibble on Diablo's mane.

"Hey, stop it," shouted Ricki, and shoved Sharazan's muzzle back. "Jake, he doesn't get enough to eat," Ricki said laughing.

"Concentrate on what's important," said the old man coldly.

Ricki sighed and devoted herself to the care of Diablo's wounds.

After about half an hour she was finished. Jake nodded his satisfaction.

"You'll be okay, Diablo. In the future, *I'll* take care of you. What happened yesterday will never happen to you again!"

Ricki was insulted and drew in her shoulders. She knew by what Jake just said that he didn't think she had been careful enough with Diablo.

Jake thought the siren was just an excuse that Lillian and Ricki made up because they didn't want to admit to him that they had failed in their responsibility to the horse.

"Jake, there really was a siren! You know how much I love Diablo. I would never—" Ricki began, but Jake turned away.

"Loving a horse and taking responsibility for him are two different things!" he answered sharply. "If I had known that you couldn't take good care of him, I would have kept Diablo myself."

Ricki eyes started to fill with tears.

"Jake, that's not fair." she responded, hurt by his remark, but the old man had already left the stable.

"Is that the way you see it, too, my boy?" she asked her horse, sniffing.

As if to answer, Diablo blew warm air gently into her hair. *Don't let it bother you,* he seemed to be saying. *I know that you told the truth. And Jake…he'll calm down again.*

"Well, come on, let's get you back to your stall," Ricki led Diablo off the corridor.

Just as she was shutting the stall gate, she heard steps on the gravel in front of the stable.

I hope he doesn't come back again, thought Ricki, who had decided to avoid Jake for the rest of the day.

"Hi, Ricki." Kevin stood in the doorway unsure of himself.

Ricki turned and stared at him.

"Kevin? What are you doing here?" I thought you were with…you were at Stony Ridge Ranch."

"I— How's Diablo? Is he really okay?" Kevin walked the corridor and looked over the top of the stall.

"My God, he looks like a patchwork quilt!"

"Do you have a spiritual connection with our vet?" asked Ricki. "He said the same thing this morning." She took out a packet of tissues from her pocket and blew her nose loudly.

"Jake thinks I'm not to be trusted with Diablo. He doesn't believe the story about the siren. I—"

"Ricki…" Kevin came up to her and apprehensively put his hands on her shoulders. "Ricki, I want to apologize to you. I was such an idiot!"

Ricki closed her eyes. "What about Melanie?" she asked.

"I already missed you on the way there. Is that enough of an answer?" Kevin tried to evade answering more directly.

"No! What about Melanie?" Ricki wouldn't give an inch.

"She is pretentious, cold, arrogant, jealous, and terribly cunning—not the sort of person that one…that I could fall in love with," Kevin tried to find the right words. "I'm *your* boyfriend…that is, if you still want me."

Ricki felt a lump in her throat and swallowed. "You're here, that says it all," she said, then turned toward him and threw her arms around his neck.

"Thank you," she said. "I'm glad you're here. I missed you, too—a lot."

Kevin smiled and embraced her.

"I never want to see Stony Ridge again," he said. "At least not without you." He kissed her lightly on the forehead and then pushed her back a bit.

"Don't be mad, but Sharazan…"

Ricki laughed, sniffing in happy tears.

"Finally, you're back to being the old Kevin!" she announced with relief.

When Lillian and Cathy had returned from their ride, they had noticed that Ricki and Kevin had made up. They were glad to see Kevin, and having the four of them together again was almost like a party.

"Kevin is back to normal again," joked Ricki, and Kevin just grinned happily.

"I think the train trip jogged my brain back in place."

"Thank heaven I called him," whispered Lillian, and Cathy gave her a friendly poke in the ribs.

"Lillian Bates, you're the best!" she grinned at her friend.

After the two horses had been taken care of, the four friends sat in front of the stable. They closed their eyes and dozed comfortably in the warmth of the sun. Each of them was still thinking about Diablo's accident and each had their own suspicions, but for the moment they avoided talking about it. After all, Diablo was doing well, considering what had happened to him, and they just wanted to enjoy the feeling that everything was okay without troublesome conversations.

"Here comes Carlotta!" Cathy announced drowsily, as she heard the sound of a car approaching.

"No," contradicted Kevin, without opening his eyes. "Carlotta's car sounds different."

"Wanna bet?" asked Cathy.

"How much?"

But Ricki interrupted the betting. "Hey, wake up. Someone's coming, but I don't recognize the car," she said quietly.

"Uh oh," said Lillian, as she saw the car. "Ricki, this is going to get difficult. That's Melanie's mother. I've seen the car at Josh's house before. Someone else is in the car, too. It's not—"

"I can't believe it!" When Ricki recognized Melanie as the passenger, she got up slowly. She stared at the approaching vehicle and her heart began to beat wildly.

"I don't know what I'll do if she has the courage to get out of the car," she said more to herself than to the others, who had gathered around her in support.

Sandra Stark let the car roll to a stop slowly. With a sideways glance at her daughter, she saw that her face was a mixture of green and white.

"Mom…I…I can't do this right now," whispered Melanie, and her voice almost broke.

144

"You're going to do it, Melanie! Ricki has a right to know, do you understand that?" said her mother firmly, and then she looked at the four young people standing in front of the stable.

"Is that the boy who invited you to that ranch for the weekend?" she asked.

Melanie nodded, alarmed.

"They're all there. They'll kill me," she whispered, slinking down in her seat. But her mother reached over and opened the car door.

"Come on now, it's not going to get any easier by putting it off."

Sandra Stark got out and then waited until Melanie got out, too, a bit awkwardly. Then she put her arm around her daughter and gently pushed her toward the four friends.

"Hello," said Melanie's mother, trying to smile. "Which one of you is Ricki?"

Without a word, Ricki took a step forward.

"Melanie has something to tell you."

Ricki started to breathe quickly. With tightly compressed lips and eyes dark with anger, she stared at Josh's cousin, who had caused Diablo so much pain.

"You actually dared to come here?" Ricki asked hoarsely, looking coldly and directly at Melanie. "After what you did? First you flirt with Kevin and act as though you're some super horseback rider, although you haven't got a clue about horses. Then you go traipsing around the stable like some prima donna, and insult your horse. And then, as though that weren't enough, you top it all off by taking your anger towards me out on my horse. What you did to Diablo, that was inhuman. You torment animals—and you're a coward, too, because otherwise you would have

145

talked to me instead of just setting off your siren, which…which—"

"I'm sorry," whispered Melanie, her eyes on the ground.

"What? What did you say?"

"Really, I never wanted—" Melanie looked pleadingly at her mother, but Sandra Stark was determined not to interfere.

"Oh, well then! You're sorry! It's a little late, I'd say, considering you found the time to go off to a riding ranch as though nothing had happened! If you didn't intend to do it, why did you do it in the first place? I'll tell you why. You thought—"

"I was furious at you," Melanie interrupted her quietly. "You were the first person who noticed that I'm afraid of horses."

"What did you say?" her mother asked, involved after all. "Why did you insist on learning to ride, then, and why did you keep nagging me to let you go on this weekend? I'd really like to know, Melanie!"

But she ignored her mother's questions. Finally, now, she was able to look Ricki straight in the eyes.

The other young people stared at her with disdain.

"You knew, or at least you thought so, the first time I came to your stable. I have no clue about riding, and certainly know nothing at all about horses. The time I spent at the stables at home was mainly in the clubhouse, not in the saddle. You can't imagine how relieved I was when Orpheus was finally tied up. I would have done anything to get out of riding back home on him. I was scared to death on the way here. Josh didn't even notice. I provoked you to get out of here. Sometimes I feel panicky around horses. I've been afraid of them for years."

Melanie paused a moment before she continued.

"I was furious because you seemed to know what I had always tried to hide… Yes, I just used Kevin to hurt you, and I thought you would break up with him after that weekend. I would never had gotten onto a horse there, I just wanted to make you jealous… but really, it's me that's jealous. Jealous of your relationship with Kevin and your friendship with your girlfriends, jealous that you all aren't afraid of horses." Melanie gulped in a breath but couldn't stop the flow of feelings that were pouring out. "I guess I just saw red. I wanted to destroy your happy life and I wanted to make you, Ricki, afraid, just once, of a horse, so you'd know what it feels like. I didn't know what I was doing when I set off the siren. When your horse was lying lifeless in the barbed wire, I somehow woke up and then ran away terrified."

Melanie's eyes filled with tears, and Ricki looked at her bewildered.

Fear of horses? Is that possible? Even Mom manages to give Diablo a carrot, thought Ricki.

"Now you know what happened," croaked Melanie. "But you have to know that I never wanted to kill your horse with that stupid plan. You have to believe me! I know that Diablo meant everything to you, and I know I can't expect you to forgive me, but please accept my apology. It's all I can do. If I could, I'd give you back your horse and undo the whole thing. I beg you, Ricki, please believe me. I'm really sincerely sorry for what I did. It's unforgivable, I know."

Melanie looked once more into Ricki's eyes, but Ricky remained silent as a stone.

Ricki's mind was racing. Melanie apparently thought

that Diablo hadn't survived the accident yesterday and seemed to be suffering because of it.

You deserve it, thought Ricki at first, but then she began to realize that Melanie wasn't actually the arrogant jerk she had pretended to be. She had just put on an act to hide her fear of horses and her insecurity around people, and the act was all anyone knew of her.

Actually, I feel sorry for her, thought Ricki. *What's important is that Diablo is alive,* she reasoned, her anger cooling. *His wounds will heal, but Melanie's fears will remain.* Then she noticed that Melanie had turned away and was crying silently.

When Ricki had still not reacted to her apology, Melanie walked back to the car with her head hanging.

"Hey," called Ricki suddenly. "Wait a minute!"

Melanie turned around slowly. With a pounding heart she watched Ricki disappear into the stable.

"I know what's going to happen," whispered Kevin to the other two girls.

"Me too," replied Lillian.

"No question about it!" confirmed Cathy.

"You have to take your hat off to Ricki," said Kevin full of admiration. "I don't think I would do it! If it were me, I'd make her suffer a little longer."

Melanie and her mother looked at each other awkwardly.

"He still has a hard time walking," Ricki's voice could be heard from inside the stable, and then she appeared in the doorway with Diablo on a lead.

Melanie looked at the horse in disbelief, thinking she was seeing a ghost.

"No!" she screamed, shaking her head, and stumbled backward. She felt as if her heart would stop.

"That's impossible, I saw him lying— Oh God, thank you!" Melanie covered her face with her hands and began to sob uncontrollably.

Her legs gave way. She sat slumped on the ground at the Sulai farm and for the first time she was not ashamed of her feelings.

Ricki was happy. Diablo was well on the way to full recovery, and as he improved, Jake's mood also improved.

One day, as they were tending to Diablo, he said to Ricki, "I didn't really mean what I said about your lack of responsibility. I was so upset about Diablo. That's why I was so grumpy," he apologized and extended his hand to her.

Ricki gave him a hug instead. "Diablo and I knew it was just because you care so much."

Three days later a huge, heavy package from Melanie arrived.

"I wonder what's in it," Ricki mused.

Lillian, who was standing around with the others, had a big grin on her face. "Ha, I know!" she said, "but I'm not telling you!"

"Well, I'm not going to guess," decided Ricki, and she began to remove the enormous amount of wrapping paper.

Finally she opened the box.

"Wow," she said in amazement as she looked inside. "A brand new saddle! Fantastic! And a letter?"

Ricki opened the envelope and began to read:

"Dear Ricki,

Thank you with all my heart for not blaming me for my un-forgivable behavior. I don't know if I would have been able to react as generously as you did.

I have bought you a saddle from my savings. I found out from Josh and Lillian that yours was damaged beyond re-pair. I hope you like it and especially that it fits Diablo. I know that nothing can replace Diablo's health, but I hope and wish I can repay you a tiny little bit with this gift.

I wish you lots of fun when you go riding in the future.

Say hello to your friends for me and give Diablo these treats from me. Tell him I think he is beautiful, even though I am afraid of him, and that it's my fault and not his that I'm afraid of horses.

Best wishes for the future,

Melanie

P.S. Mom wants you to send her the vet's bill when Diablo's treatment is completed."

Ricki slipped the letter slip into the box.

"Maybe she really is nice," she said with a smile, "but I don't plan on seeing her again, in spite of the new saddle."

Ten days after Melanie's confession, Dr. Hofer began to take out Diablo's stitches.

"Looks great," he said. "With this tough guy, every-thing's healing much faster than I thought. You'll see, Ricki, when his coat grows over the scars, they won't look half as bad."

Ricki beamed. "I'm so glad Diablo has survived every-thing relatively well and that he can finally join the other horses in the paddock."

"Yeah, it's about time that he gets some exercise. Even if he rolls around in the dirt, I don't think anything can happen now. The swelling on the pastern has gone down and he can walk almost normally. If you want, Ricki, you can take him out to join the others."

Ricki's heart leapt. Quickly she grabbed a lead, snapped it onto the halter, and within minutes was on her way to the paddock.

Dr. Hofer smiled. *Ricki and Diablo are really a great team,* he thought as he watched them.

Halfway to the paddock, the black horse stood still and whinnied to his fellow horses. His whole body was vibrating.

Look, I'm back! he seemed to say, and then he began dancing merrily beside Ricki.

"Slowly, my boy, slowly," she tried to hold her horse back and was glad when they had finally reached the paddock.

Sharazan, Rashid, Holly, and Chico were standing there to greet him, and when Ricki opened the paddock poles and snapped off the lead, Diablo raced back and forth the entire length of the paddock, joyfully kicking up his hooves. He kept going as though he wanted to prove to himself that he was completely healed.

Ricki's heart was bursting for joy.

Soon, she called to Diablo in her mind, *soon you will be able to go on rides with me, and then I promise you, my friend, we will ride to that juicy meadow near the woods. I'm sure that Mr. Anderson won't mind if you pull up a few treats for yourself. You've earned them. You're the most wonderful horse in the whole world!*